Glittering Feather

by Merri Bright

Glittering Feather

A FOREVER FEATHER NOVELLA

MERRI BRIGHT

BRIGHT AND DARK PUBLISHING

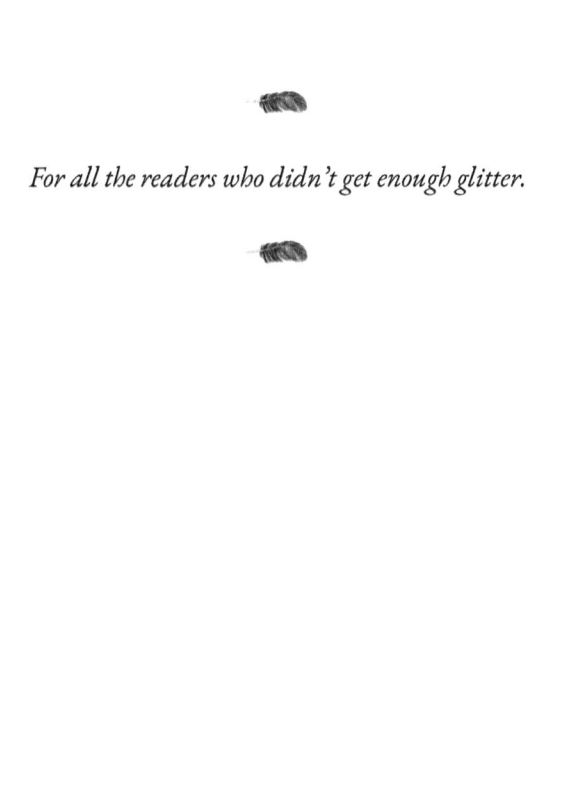

For all the readers who didn't get enough glitter.

Contents

Author's Note

Glitter*ing Feather* is humorous, steamy, glittery fun, a gift for the readers who loved *The Forgotten Angel* trilogy, and wanted more. If you haven't read those books? You'll be lost in the void on this one, birch. This novella is intended for adult readers and contains real and made-up profanity, one sexy scene, and a lot of Celestial teenaged angst. Please take care of yourself when choosing to read.

As an extra surprise, I included bonus content in the paperback. That steamy short story, *A Feather Kink*, takes place before the events in *Glittering Feather*, so I probably should have put it first. But I decided I just couldn't start with that much...macramé.

Please be aware that there is both spiritual and physical "sword crossing" (also known as m/m) in *A Feather Kink*. There's also: energy tentacle play, mention of multiple kinks, double penetration, group sex, and spiritual merging. So if you're not into that? Stop reading after Chapter 12.

Grab your kazoos one more time, birches. Shizz is about to get real in the Limen.

How hard could angelic parenting be? I had *no fudging idea*.

You'd think, with the best birches in the universe and four smoking hot angelic soulmates on my side, I could help raise one Celestial child without too much fuss.

But when the "child" is a slightly demonic teenage criminal, intent on destroying the realm to get what she wants, with an immortal canine accomplice the size of a Clydesdale, fuss doesn't come close.

Fiasco is more like it.

CHAPTER 1
Feather

The only Celestial child in existence sat on the edge of a cloud, her bare feet kicking out into the void, her charcoal gray overalls shimmering against the shining white of the improvised bench. She was singing in her raspy, alto voice like she did almost every day, though usually she made sure no one was near enough to hear.

She hated her voice.

She hated her voice, her hair, the glitter that would not come out of her skin no matter how hard she scrubbed, the way her nose turned up at the end, and how small her boobs were.

This week, she'd decided she also hated all of her dads besides Mikhail, the smell of warm chocolate, and every genre of music except something called goth trap.

But she hated me the most.

She absolutely detested the way I said "Good morning," the way my teeth clicked when I chewed, how I wore my own silver hair, the way I sneezed three times in a row "like some needy attention ho," and every other detail about me.

"Precious hates me, Sunny," I sighed, leaning into my best birch's arms. "She absolutely reviles me."

"Yes," Sunny agreed, patting my head with a hand that was sticky with something I wouldn't ask about, but hoped was caramel. "She's supposed to. She's just a teenager, and you're her mom."

"You're her mom, too, and she doesn't hate you."

"Yeah, but I'm the nice mom," Sunny gloated. "The cool mom. She has to like me more."

She was the cool mom? I'd been the one to teach Precious how to play the kazoo. I'd had Mikhail build her a playscape and a treehouse, and trees, for crying out loud. I'd convinced Gavriel to let her listen to Imriel's library of all the music that had ever existed—though if I'd known there was a goth trap song titled "My Mother Thinks She's an Angel but She's a Maggot Rat of Lies" in there, I would have reconsidered.

Sunny, the cool mom? Just because it might be true didn't mean it wasn't painful. I reached over and pinched Sunny's right nipple, hard.

"What the fu—"

"Share the pain of motherhood, birch." I glared at her. "I wrecked my spiritual vagina for that girl. I have stretch marks up and down my soul. I deserve to be the cool mom."

"Feather, you did not push her ou—" Sunny let out a frustrated shriek when I tweaked her other nipple, for symmetry. And to get her to shut up.

"Motherfuckers!" Precious had heard us and jumped up, whirling around to face us. Her long, dark purple hair, perfectly formed ebony wings, and small charcoal horns were outlined by tiny pinpricks of glitter. Her shimmering skin was gorgeous against the pure deep nothingness that stretched out behind her, and I caught my breath, like I often did, at how absolutely perfect she was.

It shouldn't have surprised me. I had named her, even if it

had been a total accident: *Precious, Perfect Devil, Little Glitter.*

But then I'd tacked on more names, when we'd come to the Limen from Sanctuary. *First and Only of Her Kind, Beloved by All Realms.* And it was that, the *Only of Her Kind* part, that made her hate me so much.

"No, sweetie," Sunny called back. "No motherfudgers. Just your mothers this time."

Precious rolled her eyes so hard it had to hurt, and turned as if to go, but Sunny flew toward her, grasping her gently below the elbow as she landed, stopping her from leaving. I ran to catch up, my stupid tiny wings flapping behind me, and reached them just as Precious stopped struggling.

"Let me go. I have to check on Shadow," she argued. It was rare to see her apart from her beloved, baby-Clydesdale-sized dog, and I wondered what had happened. "I left him shut in my room."

I chewed at my lip. That was new. And suspicious. "Why would you do that?"

"I needed to be alone." She still wouldn't look at me.

"Too bad," Sunny muttered. "We need to talk."

"I don't *want* to talk," Presh groaned as Sunny sat her forcibly back down on the cloud bench.

"No one wants this talk, Presh." Sunny's eyes met mine over my daughter's sweetly curved horns. "But it's time. We need to explain things now that you're... more mature."

Precious went still, her galaxy-colored eyes moving back and forth between us like balls in a pinball machine.

Then she snorted a laugh that echoed across the clouds around us. For a moment, I would have sworn I saw a small part of the void itself perk up, or shift, as if it was listening to her laughter.

I glared at the unmoving void until I was sure it had been only my imagination.

5

Precious was wheezing when she finally asked, "Do you mean to tell me that this is The Talk?"

When Sunny and I both nodded, Presh fell over laughing, leaving small streaks of dark purple glitter all over the surfaces around her.

Sunny held out a million-thread count handkerchief. "Wipe your face, be quiet, and listen," she ordered. "There's no way out of this conversation."

"Why now?" Presh wiped her face. "I mean, is there something going on I don't know about?"

"Yes," Sunny said, drawing out the word. "I mean, you might know."

"I'm sure you've suspected something," I added. She had been sneaking off a lot to the void edge recently, but I was sure she hadn't missed what was going on near the Celestial wall.

"Wait. This is really The Talk? And you think... I need it?" Presh stopped breathing for a second. "Is there someone who's said they might want to date me? Someone... likes me?"

"Everyone loves you, Presh," Sunny retorted. "It's literally a part of your name, Beloved of All Realms."

"Yeah, but somebody wants to *knock boots* with me?" She squealed, like this was an exciting possibility.

I hissed at the thought. She was still a child, even if she'd aged... slowly. Seraphiel had assured me that Protectors aged just like her, gradually over the course of a couple of centuries. It had been a few decades since we'd arrived in the Limen, and she still looked about seventeen or eighteen, though her adult wing feathers had finished growing in.

She and her dog Shadow were by far the youngest inhabitants of the realm, and while age gap romance was all well and good, she was my baby girl. Sure, I was an infinite number of years younger than my oldest mate, but the thought of her getting busy with a crusty old Protector... I grabbed hold of Sunny, slightly dizzy. What if she liked a *Guide*?

Oh, Great Mother of Kazoos, I should have unmade all of those perverted ashholes when I had the chance back in Sanctuary.

Sunny flicked my head. "Chill the eff out, birch. And no, Presh, there will be no knocking boots. It's just... we can't put this off any longer."

Precious slumped down, fidgeting her bare feet on the clouds. She asked in a near-whisper, "Is this because I tried to kiss Perception?"

What. The. *Fudge.* For the millionth time, I wished I could delve into my daughter's mind and see her thoughts. But she was closed to all of us. None of us were sure if she'd done it on purpose, or accidentally, but years ago her mental voice had gone silent for all of us. She said it was fair since she couldn't read our thoughts, but I was positive she'd been lying about that. I suspected she had picked up a few thoughts from some of the younger Protectors' minds before. Either that or she'd forced secrets out of them in some more nefarious way.

Beside me, Sunny was losing her shit, her wings flaring. "I'll fucking kill him," she raged. "He never said a word. He knew I'd unmake him; that's why."

Precious curled up into a ball. She was trembling. Was she *crying*?

Sunny, chill. Something's wrong, I thought, wrapping an arm around my daughter's shaking wings. "He didn't tell us anything about it. Should he have?"

"Why would he?" she said at last. "It's not like he kissed me back. I thought he was going to tear his lips off after."

"What happened, baby?" I breathed.

"He didn't know who I was at first. It was dark. When he saw who it was, he was disgusted. He said he hadn't consented. That he thinks I'm a ch-child with no impulse control." She burst into tears then, and Sunny and I both wrapped our arms around her, holding her as she wept. I could barely make out

7

her words, but I tried to put together her meaning from the fragmented, sobbing confession.

Of the two of us, Sunny was surprisingly the more contained at the end of Precious's meltdown. "So after your classes were over yesterday, instead of coming home, you hid by the hot springs near the Celestial wall until it was dark. You waited until Perception got into the water, and then you slid in behind him," she restated calmly. But Sunny's calm was the terrifying kind, like when the eye of a hurricane is directly overhead. "He was naked, yes?"

Precious nodded.

"And you were wearing *what*?"

She hiccupped. "The swimsuit I was born in?" she said, like it was a question.

There was no visible wind, but glitter swirled all around us in an angry tornado, the tiny particles stinging my skin. I glared out at the void, wondering where that had come from.

"He should have told us," Sunny said aloud once she'd gotten control of herself. "Hope and I will be having words with that man."

Precious shrieked. "Oh my glitter, no! Tata, I will literally die of shame." She pulled away from Sunny and clung to me like a purple barnacle.

I melted into her arms, soaking up the unusual affection. "Sunny, I think you should go. Get dinner ready. I'll talk to Presh about the other thing." *Catch up with Percy and find out what the heck happened.*

Absofuckinglutely, she agreed, and flew away.

Precious and I sat there, awkwardness setting in as usual. But when I held out a hand, she took it. "So, that was your first kiss, huh?"

"Yeah," she muttered. "And I know I shouldn't have done it, I do. But for, like, that one tiny moment, I felt like that part of me that hurts all the time, didn't hurt so much."

I let my other hand rise to rest on her wing, on the place where she had one missing feather. It had fallen out—or been plucked—years before, when we'd first left Sanctuary. We didn't talk about it often, but all of her parents were worried about what it meant that she felt pain every day. Especially after she'd admitted to Hope a few months before that it was getting worse.

I was almost certain it was part of why she was always in a foul mood. It wasn't like Protectors had hormones. Although, she was the only one of her kind, so who knew what was normal.

"It didn't even last a second," she said, slanting a glance at me. "It probably doesn't even count as a first kiss."

I smiled weakly. I wasn't going to get into the ins and outs of non-consensual kissing. I already knew her Papa Gavriel would take point on that conversation. "I get it. You're lonely. You want someone to love."

"Yeah. Or even just Netflix and chill with." I threw up in my mouth a little bit at that, but before I could ask where she'd heard that expression, she went on. "So if it wasn't the thing with Perception, what were you coming to talk to me about?"

Oh boy. This was going to get ugly.

"You know the new building we've all been working on?" The senior Guides and Protectors had been pooling our energy for the past few months to work on the project. A little piece of Sanctuary in the Limen, and it was almost done. Only none of us had talked to Precious about what it was. She hadn't paid much attention, and when she'd asked Mikhail what he was spending so much time on, he'd called it a "community hall."

"Yeah, what about it?"

"Well, it's almost finished, and..." *Oh, fudge me sideways.* She was going to hate me even more once I told her what her dads and moms had all agreed on. "It's not really a, uh, community center. Precisely."

"What is it?" Her eyes narrowed. "If it's another school building, I swear I'll burn it down." Tiny sparks shot from her eyes.

"You said that was an *accident*, Presh," I growled. "Don't tell me you wasted all that energy to get out of going to classes —" I gasped when her left eye twitched. It was her tell. We had questioned her very thoroughly the year before, when the school building had caught fire right before her Earth History from the Jurassic to the Present final exam. I'd been sure she'd done it on purpose. She was my daughter, after all, and I would have burned down the entire realm if I'd had to sit exams like that. She'd vowed that she hadn't.

But Precious had a few traits that no one else in the Limen had. Perfect Devil as she was, she could lie very effectively, without anyone knowing. Anyone except... "Did Perception know?"

She shrugged, but her cheeks went even more glittery.

"Why, Presh?" She tried to pull her hand away, but I held on. "I won't tell." She sneered, and I squeezed her hand tighter. "I swear on all the glitter in the universe, I will not tell a soul." I closed off my mental lines of communication with my mates and hoped they wouldn't go probing around in these memories. "Why did you do it?"

"He was doing private tutoring with her," she said after a long moment. "With Adoration." Her chin trembled. "He had Tradition giving me all those tests, and I had to re-take them when I failed, and I was failing *everything* because I couldn't focus when I kept hearing him in the next room over with *her*. Even when I asked him to help me study, he told me no. *She* was the one he wanted to be with."

She held out her arm, turning it to catch the early morning light from the Celestial Realm. The smears of smut and glitter she'd carried around her entire life made patterns like an Impressionist masterpiece on her skin. "I'm evil, and ugly, and stupid, Mom. I didn't mean to burn it down. I just got mad, and when I do, bad things happen."

My heart broke into a million pieces as she dissolved into sobs again. I rocked her back and forth, even though she had been too big to hold on my lap for years now. When had she gotten so big? When had she lost sight of how perfect and unique she was?

"I think Adoration is a total skank, you know," I whispered in her ear when she quieted down. "She's desperate. She throws herself at a lot of Protectors, even some Guides. I saw her flirt with *Fidelity*."

We both said, "Ewwww!" at the same time, then laughed.

She sniffled, wiped her face on the front of her overalls, and tried to smile. "So, what about the community center?"

I sighed. "It's not a community center."

"Nice try, Mom. Dad can't tell a lie." She screwed up her nose. "Or at least, he wouldn't. Baba Rumple would, maybe..."

I fidgeted. "Fine, it's *sort of* a community center. For special, um, groups. And group activities." She was glaring at me again, and I let out a breath. "Precious, when a Protector, or even a Guide, and another Protector or Guide... or even a whole group of them... love each other, very, very much, and want to show that love in a physical and spiritual fashion—"

"It's a sex club?" Her eyes went so big, I could see planets and distant suns moving inside them. "They're building a new Merge?"

"Yes," I said slowly, wondering who in the helter-skelter had told her about the old Merge back in Sanctuary. "But it's for adults only. No one under two hundred is allowed to enter."

She let out a string of curse words so filthy, I could see the smut accumulate on her face like someone was splattering her with a paintbrush. "Who made *that* rule? You? Papa Gavriel? Tata Sunny?"

"We all did," I told her as she wrenched away. Desperate, I rushed on, regretting my words even as they flooded out. "But if you'd like to take a peek inside... it's not opening until tomorrow. We can sneak in?"

In a split second, her curses turned to compliments, and her attitude to praise.

Ha. Who's the cool mom, now? I thought as we raced over the cloud ground to the site of the only forbidden part of the Limen for my precocious, perfect child.

I wasn't sure why, but in the distant part of the void, I could have sworn I heard mocking laughter.

CHAPTER 2

Feather

"What are they going to call it?" Precious whispered as we entered the new "community hall." We'd tiptoed through the back entrance into the main dance hall—a room the size of a fancy concert hall, but lacking seats.

Well, there were sex chairs all around the perimeter of the room, and a few plush sofas in blue and gold velvet and leather, with an eye-opening number of golden grommets for the chains and ropes that would be brought in later. But nothing else. I hoped Presh didn't notice the hardware.

I sure as heck hoped no one had realized where we were.

Gavriel was going to lecture me until I'd want to be unmade.

Mikhail wouldn't be mad, just disappointed.

Righteous would remind me in his best Head Boy voice that we'd all agreed as a group not to allow her inside, and then he'd probably schedule another boring family meeting.

Rumple would laugh, but possibly spank me after the meeting, which didn't exactly inspire me to back us out of the room.

I waved at the wall where a sign had been constructed,

with the words *Welcome to* painted in glitter and gold over a blank swath of marble, where the club's name would go. Mikhail was going to bring the naming chime out and do a public dedication, finishing the sign and the club for the grand opening.

There was only one problem.

"They have no idea what name to pick," I replied, opening my thoughts just enough to make sure no one was here. Mikhail had been working all hours of the day and night, trying to ensure every detail was right.

Over the past ten years or so, some of the approximately two thousand refugees in the Limen—mostly the longer-lived residents of Sanctuary, who had grown used to their creature comforts—had grown increasingly depressed. This space wasn't just for group sex and kinky fuckery. It was a sacred space.

"It's a holy place," I breathed, my voice echoing to the top of the vaulted ceiling.

"Um, maybe a place to get your holes filled," Precious muttered.

"On that topic..." I slid down on one of the sex chairs, folding my tiny wings in the gaps provided for just that. "Have a seat and let's get this over with."

"You don't need to give me The Talk." She rolled her eyes, but crossed her own legs and sat on the floor nearby, picking at some of the flecks of glitter that were everywhere in this realm. "I know all about P in the V. Or P in the A. Or two Ps in the V and one in the A—"

"Oh, Great Maker of All Sausages, please stop talking," I groaned. "That's not The Talk. And also, I told you to stop sneaking into my private library." I glared at her, and she slumped down. "Those books are fiction anyway, my little glitter baby."

"I figured," she said with a curled lip. "There's no way you could fit that many sausages into one bun."

"Totally. Physically impossible," I lied.

Both her eyebrows flew up. She might be able to hide her thoughts and lie to us, but the reverse was not at all true.

"Without vast quantities of lube," I finished, and she made a face. I rushed on before she could ask the questions that I could tell had started forming about lube. "I want to talk to you about merging. Not just physical stuff, but the spiritual side of things."

"Okay," she said cautiously. "What about it?"

"So, merging is physical, mental, and spiritual. When two souls merge, they—how did you put it? Knock boots in the V? Play side pocket pool with the P and A? Whatever. But that's not the most important part. The best part of merging is the way your spirit moves into the one you're merging with. You open yourself up completely to them, and they open themself to you. You don't have any secrets, or hidden places. You're completely connected to one another."

"That's what they're going to do in here?" She stared at the sex chairs, definitely noticing the grommets and hardware. "Wait. So people only spiritually merge with, like, mates, right? That's good." She shuddered. "I can't imagine wanting to be that exposed with a bunch of randos."

Her jaw dropped when I shook my head. "No, Presh. People open themselves up to others they're attracted to. Not just chosen mates. You have to remember—the rest of us, our minds are kind of open a lot of the time already. It's not that scary to open them up a little mo—"

"Is *he* going to come here?" she demanded, standing, sparks flying from her whirling eyes. "Does he think he's going to come in here and merge? With someone like her, someone prettier and older and more perfect... Is he planning to touch her?" Her wings flared out, each feather glowing with dark fire. The floor directly beneath her feet began to bubble, like it was melting. "Fucking *Adoration*?"

I jumped out of my chair. "Precious, stop it!" If she kept going like this, she'd melt a hole through the entire Limen. Her flames burned hotter than Celestial fire, and putting them out took an immense amount of power. I thought about mentally calling for Rumple. He was often the only one she'd listen to when she got this way, and possibly the only one who could extinguish the blaze if it got going.

"Time to count, baby," I whispered desperately. I wanted to take her hands and talk her down, but if I touched her now, she might burn me, too.

She nodded almost imperceptibly, holding still.

"You're talking about Perception, aren't you?" I said quietly as she closed her eyes, fighting to regain control of her volatile emotions.

Eyes still closed, she muttered a "yes" between inaudible numbers. The floor was beginning to cool down, turning black instead of ember-red. "Mom. I... I love him. I want to be with him."

My stomach dropped. This was a crush that we'd all seen coming, but knew had no future. How could I make her see? "You have to understand, sweetheart. He's a grown Protector. He was your teacher once. He can't... He can't ever merge with you."

She put her hands over her face, so I almost couldn't make out her next words. "He wouldn't want to, anyway. If merging is what you say... if it means he'd see inside me? I would never want him to. I never want him to know what I'm really like." Her last words ended on a choked-off sob as she sank to her knees.

"What do you mean?" I whispered.

"I'm evil, Mom." Her voice was a low rasp. When she finally lifted her eyes to my face, I had to force myself not to react. The swirling galaxies that were so entrancing had changed. They were dark, and bottomless, like the Abyss itself. "I'm evil to my core."

"You are perfect as you are," I replied firmly, wishing I could force her to believe it. To see it. "It's in your name."

"Yeah, Mom. Perfect Devil. Thanks for that." Her nostrils flared as she sneered again, putting on her teenage attitude armor like it would protect her from the emotions that raged inside her.

Before I could speak, a baying hound came racing through the open door of the hall and skidded to a stop on chocolate-stained paws, right next to Precious. He licked her face, tasting her tears.

For a moment, Shadow stared at me with a question in his wise doggy eyes. I shook my head, and he lay over my daughter's lap, flopping down for pats. His enormous, hematite-gray body almost completely obscured hers.

"Can you go?" Presh asked, her voice still tear-choked. "I want to be alone."

Leaving her alone and heartbroken was the last thing I wanted to do. My daughter was alone far too often, and I worried that she would spiral deeper into her sadness.

But when she added a soft "please," I murmured my agreement. "Of course. I'll walk you outside, sweetie." Shadow jumped up and tugged on her sleeve. She didn't take the arm I offered, but she followed me through the back door and slumped to a seat on a nearby bench. I nodded to Shadow, but I already knew he would stay with her.

I wasn't certain there was any power in the universe strong enough to separate him from his beloved friend for more than a few hours.

I hoped there wasn't.

My own house wasn't that far from the community hall, but it took a lot longer when your wings were stupidly tiny and you had to walk. I was about halfway back when the hottest Protector in the Limen flew directly overhead and hovered there. I stared up at his dangling bits, that were really less "bits" and more "lengths of thick pipe" that grew thicker and more prominent as I gawked.

"Scrap, are you staring up my robe again?" the dark-haired hottie called down.

I kept staring. "I don't know, Anaconda Pants, are you hovering over me because you're some kind of super-powered flasher who gets your kicks surprising poor, unsuspecting women with peeks at your Megalodon Peen?" The clouds around me jiggled slightly with his laughter.

"I'll give you more than a peek if you vote for my name for the community hall," he cajoled as he landed next to me. I jumped up into his arms, and he flew us back toward the house.

"What's your current pick for a name? If you let me paint you with chocolate and lick it off while Rumple watches—"

"*Tied up* Rumple?" Righteous interrupted. His cheeks were slightly rosy. Tied up Rumple was a particular favorite in our bedroom.

"Sure," I said with a shrug. "I'll throw in Rumple in ropes with the chocolate art lesson. Tell me what you want to call it first, though."

He grinned. "Mine is the best. I was thinking the Sanctified Sexposium."

I wrinkled my nose. "Ew. No. That sounds like a strip joint near a regional airport. Try again."

"It's alliterative! It's descriptive! What's wrong with it?" he muttered as he flew. "It's better than Mik's idea. The Spiritual Cloisters? Way too formal and religious. Gavriel suggested the

Consortium." We both wrinkled our noses. "Rumple's latest was Heavenly Bodies."

That wasn't terrible, but still. Kind of low-rent gentlemen's club.

"Why can't we just call it The Merge Two: Electric Boogaloo, like I want?" I grumbled as he set me down outside our door.

"Because we'll have to live with it for eternity—or at least until balance is restored in the entire universe and the Celestial Realm gate opens up." Righteous tapped my nose with one finger. "By the way, if anyone asks, I cheered you up."

"You did?" I put my hands on my hips, giving him my best skeptical glare.

He put his hands on my hips, and his lips on mine, and for a few moments, blew all my cares away in a swirl of rose-scented passion.

I slumped against him when he tried to pull away. "Did Growly tell you I was sad?"

"No one had to tell me. I felt it." He placed a hand over the feather-shaped mating mark on his arm. I felt an answering pulse of warmth in the feather he had given me, wrapped around my right nipple.

"Calm down, Esther," I whispered to my boob.

"Are you all right now?" Ry asked gently. "You know it scares me when you shut down our connection."

According to Ry and Mikhail, it was more than scary. It reminded them of the weeks when I was apart from them, and had almost died. Well, actually died. But I tried not to think about my vast history with all of the dying and being reborn.

"Sorry, yes. I had to cut you all off for just a little bit. Presh had secrets. Girl talk," I specified when Righteous's bright golden eyes narrowed. He curled those impossibly beautiful lips in a suspicious smirk. I jumped up and kissed him one more time before rushing inside.

Other than Righteous and me, the house was empty. I picked up faint traces of music from Gavriel—who was most likely in his music room out the back—along with a feeling of dissatisfaction from Rumple, and a deep current of worry from Mikhail.

I sent out a thought that I needed them.

None of them replied.

What the actual fudgesicle? Was this what people meant when they said the bloom had gone off the rose? Or was it the shine off the apple? No, wait, when the lube was off the tentacle dildo.

Whatever, it *hurt*.

They thought they could ignore me? I closed my eyes, grabbed the cords that stretched between us all with mental fists of fury, and sent a shouted mental command down the lines to all my mates as I also yelled the words, *"HAREM, ASSEMBLE!"*

I heard shouts, squawks, what might have been a kazoo, and Righteous next to me, rolling around on the floor and holding his head like I'd shouted right into his ear... *Wait.* I had done that. "Sorry, Ry."

He gave a weak thumbs-up and was almost back on his feet when the others barreled into the front room.

"Sweet soul, what happened?" In a second, Mikhail had me in his arms, his scarred hands running up and down my body, checking for injuries. His hands were warm and smelled slightly of bread dough. He'd been baking again. Yum.

I went limp as he ran those sensitive, muscular fingers up and over the tips of my wings, cataloging every feather and sending quivers of desire to my lady parts. Double yum.

"Are you hurt, beloved?"

"Maybe. Check some more. Check a little lower," I whimpered, as Gavriel reached around and grasped my chin in one hand, angling my face to his.

"She's not hurt, Mik. She's just being a brat." Gavriel's blue and gold eyes bored into mine with a promise of future punishment.

My lady bits did an invisible fist pump.

"Little Sacrifice, you called?" Rumple's velvety-smooth voice emerged from the doorway. "It's not the best time." It wasn't his words, but his thoughts that had us all turning to examine him.

In his hand, he had something small and golden... and melted.

"What is *that?*" Righteous gasped.

Gavriel stepped closer. "Who did that?"

"Oh shizzcrickets," I whispered as Rumple held up what was unmistakably the naming chime.

It had been a golden, clapperless bell, small enough to fit in the palm of my hand. Powerful enough that Mikhail had used it to create everything in the Limen, using the energy that Imriel, the leader of the Celestial Realm, had somehow managed to push through the barrier between realms to us.

The chime had been the tool used to give names to almost every Protector that existed, connecting a new soul with their truest name—their destiny, almost. But now it was melted.

Ruined.

"What happened to it?" Gavriel demanded. "Who would have... It was in Mikhail's workshop."

"I found it in Precious's room, stuffed under Shadow's bed," Rumple said softly, as Mikhail let out a soft, keening wail and grabbed the lump of metal from his hand.

"Why?" Righteous breathed, as we all stood in shock and horror. "Why would she have done this?"

My heart felt like it was being squeezed in an invisible fist, when Rumple answered, "I think I know. But I don't want to say."

CHAPTER 3
Seraphiel

As the First of the Celestial Children, I had lived for countless millennia and seen destruction in all its forms. The small, ruined bell that my heart friend Mikhail held and mourned now was nowhere near the worst. But it might be the most painful for the inhabitants of our in-between realm.

Living here in the Limen, sandwiched between the void and the Celestial Realm that was our rightful home, the naming chime had made it possible to create some semblance of comfort. To build the trappings of home around us.

We could still eat, since the energy we consumed came from the upwelling springs in the cloud surfaces nearest the Celestial Realm. But beyond that... I felt the eyes of my family on me as I pressed my lips together, not wanting to share what I'd sensed in the naming chime. The past that I'd read in it.

Righteous broke the silence. "Mikhail? Can you make another one?"

The burly High Angelus folded his bronze wings close, glanced at me, then shook his head. "I wouldn't want to. The making of a new chime? It's not worth the sacrifice."

I agreed immediately. "Great Singer, no. Never again."

What sacrifice? I heard my small, beautiful mate's question in my thoughts and slammed every door of my mind shut on the memories of what had gone into the creation of this one. If anyone would try to forge a new one, regardless of the cost, it would be Feather.

She must never learn of this, I sent on narrow threads of thought to Gavriel, then Mikhail, while Righteous distracted Feather with murmured questions.

Agreed, they sent back immediately.

I felt a sharp pain on my shin and looked down. "Little Sacrifice, did you kick me?"

"I know you're talking about me," she growled, her green eyes crackling like emeralds on fire. "Or telling secrets. You know that won't end well for you."

Gavriel and Mikhail started coughing, while Righteous gulped audibly. "Hey, I wasn't in on it—"

She cut him off with a glance. "Don't act like you weren't already planning to be. Tell me what happened to the chime." *You don't need to tell me how to fix it,* she added mentally, with a shudder. *I could never do that.*

How did you—? I cursed mentally, then wrapped my arms around her. She grabbed hold of my golden tail and tucked it between us, as she liked to do when she needed comfort. *I didn't want you to see that memory, little one.*

I glanced at our other mates, who all reached out to touch Feather, comforting her while I searched for the tendril of her soul that had obviously worked its way past my inner defenses. She was still there, her golden soul shining brighter than my own inner light, staring at the memory from the day Sanctuary was sealed.

"Revel. Brother." *I whispered his true name in my mind.* Revelation of Divine Mysteries. *"If I do this, I don't know when*

I'll be able to change your form back. This place needs a bridge—"

"Yes," Revel agreed, his dark eyes shining from his equally dark, gloriously beautiful face. He was smiling, as always.

Revel's smile was a constant in my universe. Even when his mouth wasn't visible, an eternal dance of humor, curiosity, and mystery shone in his eyes. As if the entirety of Her creation had been revealed to him, and he was keeping the gleeful secret from all of us.

"Oh, I love that dream," Revel said, throwing his arms around me. His wings were as ebony-dark as the rest of him, and just as perfect. "That's exactly what it's like. Although not always joyful. Mother's secrets aren't necessarily dipped in sweetness." A flash of pain flitted behind his eyes. "I know I'll be the bridge for a long time. It's where I need to be."

I sighed. Revel had embodied his nickname for too long. He was the consummate flirt, exuding divine charisma, and he'd merged with at least half the Celestial Realm. His constant focus on pleasure had resulted in him being perceived as a hedonist, if one of the First Children could be imagined as such. The censure of the others had drained him of some of his joy, and I suspected his desire to commit to becoming the bridge between realms was an effort to change that perception.

"You know those who love you, and know you best, see your heart, Revel. You don't need to change for anyone."

His fathomless eyes shone with a holy fervor. "I know. But it's also where she needs me to be."

"She?" Something prickled in my soul. A premonition. I saw a young woman, dark winged and dark eyed, with shimmering skin, and evil surrounding her on all sides. Lost, trapped, crying for him. For Revel. "You don't mean our Mother. You mean someone else."

"Well, Mother, too," he replied, stepping back into the clouded space we'd created, the final place that would separate

Sanctuary, this place of learning and growth for all the children of our kind, from the gathering darkness of the Abyss. "I will be a bridge for as long as the Maker of Mysteries needs. And then... I'll be something else. She hasn't shared what, but I can tell it will be worth the wait."

"I still don't understand how," I began, uncertain how to state my doubts. Revel had always been the least serious of all our siblings. The most likely to leave a task undone, to dance away from his work and fall into the lustful embrace of others. "How can you be certain you won't move? Crumble? The pressure from the void, the strain of holding the realms apart... You're strong, but—"

"Not the strongest of our siblings," he laughed. Then he laughed again, as if he were savoring the sound. "No. The younger shouldn't be, should he? But I can become as strong as I need to be. All it takes is a little sacrifice." His breath caught, as if on a sob. "Remind me of that. Please. Sing it to me, later. That the little sacrifice will release me."

Little sacrifice? Those two words sent me to my knees, though I had no understanding of why. "Remind you? Revel?"

His hands landed on my head, and he lifted my face to his. Tears streaked down his cheeks, the air around us suddenly filling with the scent of lilies. "I have to let my memory of the deepest mysteries go, if I am to change."

I held up my hands and caught the tears as they fell, as he sang a Naming Song that stripped away his identity. Transformed it. When I could stop weeping, I sang along, harmonizing with him.

Eternal Bridge. Great Conduit. "Great Gate," he rasped as we both stared down into my hands.

The tears I'd caught had formed a small, golden, bell-shaped lump in my hands. It was warm, soft, and infinitely precious.

"I take my strength into my new life," my youngest brother

who had been Revel said, as he stepped back and began to change. He grew taller and wider, and began to glow, as golden as the bell in my hands. He lifted his hands high, stretching his wings, which began to unfurl into golden arches and swirls, filling the one gap in the realm we'd spent so long forming together.

"I leave with you the joyful secrets of Her great plans. The dance of Her unfurling light. The melody of Her greatest truths. And my knowledge of the end of my own story, dearest Seraphiel."

"I'll miss dancing with you, Revel."

"Will you sing to me?" he asked, his tone strained. "Sing to me, so I don't forget myself entirely?"

"Of course I will. Every day. I will sing all our songs." The songs of making and naming and joy.

He blinked, and his eyes grew troubled. "Seraphiel. What's happening? I can't see. It's so cold. What have I done? I can't—" His lips moved, but no sound emerged. His skin changed, losing its perfect dark hue, and turned paler, bleaching into a golden swath. An almost punishing heat emanated from the surface of it, and it took all my resolve not to step back from it.

But he had given up so much to play his part in the making of this realm. The least I could do was stand watch, to witness his sacrifice. And sing.

Let it not be forever, Mother, *I prayed with my melody.* Let him not be separated from us for long. *The small bell grew cooler in my hands, and I felt a pang in the well of my soul.*

It would be a very, very long time before I danced with my brother again.

He became a gate. I stood, weeping, watching, as the physical form my brother had worn for millennia altered entirely. At last, after what felt like an agonizing eternity, the metal surface —shimmering with movement as if a great wind blew behind it —grew cool enough to approach. There were fields there, wide and waving with grain. Mountains in the distance, and a sky filled with storm clouds.

And a small, winged form clutching his head in his hands, staring up at me, his mouth moving, no sounds emerging.

But each time the figure tried to speak, the small chime in my hand hummed.

"It was his voice?" Feather asked quietly, taking the ruined bell from Mik's hand gently, as if she held a newborn chick.

"More than that, I think. It was his knowledge of Her divine mysteries. Or at least, many of them. I know that after Revel became the Great Gate, he didn't understand... why he had done it. Not precisely. I explained as much as I knew, but he had never told me all of it. Revel was a joker, a trickster. He liked to keep secrets, and it was his nature to tease us with the very best ones." I sighed deeply. "The first new souls I created in Sanctuary—with the help of Mikhail's Master, the original Maker in that realm—were formed while we still didn't understand how to use the chime. We experimented, and ended up having to rename a few of the earliest souls."

Feather's eyes grew wide. "You got their names wrong? And just... renamed them? And you gave me so much shizz about Precious!"

"You named her after the One Ring of Power, forged in secret in the fires of Mount Doom, you beautiful brat," Mikhail grumbled. "I'm sure whatever mistakes Seraphiel made, they weren't that bad."

I laughed. "Not nearly." We all grew silent, staring at the chime. "But that's why I'm certain Precious was the one to do this." Pain resonated through all our mating bonds, and the mating feathers in my flesh constricted slightly.

"But why?" Gavriel asked quietly, his hand on his chest. "What was she trying to make?"

"She wasn't making anything, was she?" Feather whispered, her voice catching. She held up the chime, examining it closely. "She is the child of the Maker, after all."

"I think she was trying to change something." I shook my head. That would not have resulted in this much destruction. "Possibly she was attempting to remake something..." I didn't want to finish my sentence, since I knew how terribly it would hurt our little mate. Feather's heart was softer than ever, as if motherhood had altered her fundamentally.

Our daughter's presence had changed all of us.

When the answer came, it was Feather who spoke it, her voice filled with pain. "She was trying to remake herself. Change her name. And it's my fault."

CHAPTER 4
Mikhail

"Sweet soul, no," I murmured, gathering my small mate into my arms, the searing pain where her mating feather lay throbbing like a sudden wound. She wept for a few moments, and I silently alerted the others. *Gav, let the others know the naming ceremony for the hall will be delayed. No need to tell them why just yet. Righteous, go tell Sunny and Hope what we found. Seraphiel? Find our child. Keep her safe.*

They all nodded. In a flurry of wings that had loose glitter swirling around the room, they were gone in seconds.

Feather's soft cries cut into my heart like invisible soul knives. "Hush, my beloved. Quiet now. You did nothing wrong when you named our daughter. And nothing wrong when you renamed her."

Feather hiccuped against my chest and mumbled, "Don't lie, Growly. You'll get smutty."

"I'm not lying." I carried her to the bed, setting her down gently. "Were you lying to me when you said you forgave me for renaming you Useless? No, it was worse than that. Useless Scrap. Did I deserve to suffer for my mistake?"

"No." She squeezed me in a fierce hug.

"You renamed yourself in the void, with Seraphiel. You did a very good job of it. And when you added onto Precious's name when we came here, you did well again. You gave her strength, connection, and love with that name."

"You really think so?"

"I know so. Let us hope that Precious is just going through what parents on Earth would call a phase. That horrible time in adolescence when you dislike everything about yourself." I wasn't certain I believed this myself, but I needed to soothe my little mate.

"You're not mad at her for breaking your chime?"

"I'm disappointed that she felt the need to steal it from my workshop. Devastated that she's been suffering, with none of us aware of how low her self-esteem has become. But she is my daughter. I would sacrifice every tool I've ever touched, and everything I've created, to secure her happiness. She is precious to me beyond all comprehension."

Feather hiccupped as she stared at the remnant of the naming chime. "The name of my daughter is Precious," she stated clearly.

The chime remained silent.

"We're both Namers," she whispered. "Maybe if we try together."

I wrapped her small hand in mine, and we both repeated the words.

The chime stayed quiet.

Then she squeezed her hand around mine and said, "The name of our daughter *was* Precious."

My fingers vibrated as the chime resonated with a faint, sour tone.

"I think it does still work," Feather gasped.

I held my breath. Had Precious succeeded in renaming herself?

And if she had, what had she chosen?

"Remember when you were trying to find my whole name? And the chime would ring a little, until you got all of the parts? What if she just added to it? What if most of it is the same?"

"She's not here," I said, stroking my chin. "It works best when the person is present."

"But we're both Namers, right?"

I nodded slowly. "It should answer us, even without her here. In Sanctuary, when I needed to uncover facets of a true name for one of the new Protectors, it would hum lightly when I found the next part of a true name."

"Then this might work." She leaned over her cupped hands, taking a deep breath.

I wanted to ask Feather not to say our daughter's full name aloud, not to discover if she had done something irreversible, but my little mate was braver than any soul I'd ever known. She stuck out that pointed stubborn chin and said clearly, directing her words at the chime, "Our child is... Precious, Perfect Devil, Little Glitter, shiny, and lovely, and stubborn. First and Only of her Kind; Beloved by All Realms; Guarded by the Great Gate; Protected by Sunny, the Light of Truth; my daughter, and that of Mikhail the Great-Souled, Maker of Sanctuary."

When she finished, a strange, dissonant, doubled tone hummed from the lump, almost inaudible, but there. I held my breath, listening to the odd sound, uncertain what that meant.

Perhaps, if we held it over Precious herself and tried again, we could discern exactly what she had done. Maybe I could fix it. Change it back...

"Growly?" Feather's question interrupted my train of thought. "Does it sound that way because she did rename herself? Or because it's broken?"

"I don't know." I held her hand up, examining the molten,

buckled edges of the tool I'd used my entire life to create. It wasn't gone, but this was almost worse. I knew without asking that nothing I made using this would ever be exactly right.

The familiar glint of stubbornness filled Feather's eyes before she stated, "I am Feather, the Beautiful Sacrifice, Beloved of Mikhail the Great-Souled, Maker of Sanctuary; best friend to Sunny, The Light of Truth, Ride or Die Birch; Treasured Little One of Seraphiel, known as Rumple, my Teacher and First Love; Secret Crush of Righteous Arm of Justice, Head Protector of Sanctuary who shall henceforth be known as Anaconda Pants; and Chief Antagonist and Adored Nemesis of Gavriel the Grumpy Lightbearer; Leader of Sanctuary."

The chime let out a single note that ended on what was possibly the worst sound it had ever emitted.

"Did it... Did it just... fart?" Feather glared at the chime, but in seconds, one corner of her lips was twitching.

I stated my name. "I am Mikhail the Great-Souled..." When I finished, the chime made an even louder farting noise, and a tiny puff of air seemed to come from the center of the chime.

"Oh, this can't be good," Feather groaned, holding up her palm for me to see. It was covered with flecks of dark purple and charcoal gray glitter. "She really, really broke it."

"Yes, she did." I had no idea what the foul sound or glitter meant, and I wasn't certain why it made me feel slightly better. Almost... amused? Like this was all just some great cosmic joke being played out, and I was waiting for the punchline.

My mind spun with the ramifications of losing a working chime. We weren't done building in the Limen. We had all the energy we needed, since we could consume the energy that welled up through the cloud ground, courtesy of Imriel and the Celestial Realm. But not to be able to create with the chime... it would be a devastating blow to the morale of our populace. Our friends.

And what would my purpose be here if I couldn't *make*? I was a Maker...

"On a scale of one to Righteous with no lube, where are we sitting, Papa Bear?" Feather's gaze snagged me, pulling me out of the unusual spiral of self-pity that had threatened.

I closed her fingers over the chime. "We are sitting in the same place we were before we discovered this. The community hall is finished, more or less, though we'll need to cancel the naming ceremony for now. We all have homes, except for a few of the younger Protectors, like your friend Truth in the Smallest Detail."

"And Truth and his naked octet *like* shacking up in one room, so they won't be upset," she replied, wrapping her arms around me in a much less desperate embrace. "You're right. And you can make some tools with the energy and your singing, right? You don't have to have the chime?"

I laughed loud and long. "You're absolutely correct, sweet soul. In fact, my Master forced me to learn my craft for centuries without any access to that powerful tool. It's just been so long since I had to create polished works without its help to center their purpose, I've gotten spoiled." I found myself grinning. "It might even be fun. I could teach Gavriel how to do it as well. He'll need new instruments at some point. He'll need to learn how to create them from raw energy."

Feather's wicked laugh matched mine, and before I knew it, we were embracing, our souls swirling around each other like twin flashes of lightning racing from one soul well to the other.

"You make me feel young," I murmured, smiling down at her clouded gaze, her kiss-swollen lips. I was glad I'd been able to distract her. Keeping my little soulmate happy was something I could do, with or without a chime.

"Well, you *are* an old man. You'd better be thankful I had a hidden daddy kink," she muttered.

"Hidden?" I teased as we heard Gavriel's mental call, and went to join him in the small park I'd created between our house and Sunny and Hope's. "You thought you'd hidden it?"

"I have unplumbed depths, Grandpa," she sassed. "Whole vistas of unexplored sexual desires."

"If the four of your mates haven't filled your holes and plumbed your depths by now, birch, you may need to reconsider your mate bonds," a sultry voice interrupted.

"Hope!" Feather shouted, throwing herself into Hope's arms, while Sunny and I exchanged concerned glances. Gavriel and Righteous were seated on the bench by the playscape, both of them morose. Gavriel had an arm around Righteous, and the juxtaposition of their golden and dark beauty made me want to paint them like this.

"Where is she?" I asked Sunny.

"Precious flew off. Seraphiel's gone to find her."

"Good." I settled cross-legged on the ground by the bench, and they all joined me in a circle, rehashing the implications of what had happened, and hoping we would find the right approach to help our troubled girl learn to love herself.

CHAPTER 5

Feather

"We're going to ground her until she's eighty-five," Hope announced a few moments into our group discussion about the consequences of Precious's actions. "It's the only way."

"That seems a bit harsh," Mikhail grumbled as he pressed close to me. When I patted his hand and ran the backs of my nails over the mark on his arm where my mating feather rested, he went quiet.

Gavriel sank down on my other side and began finger-combing my messy hair, picking the occasional stray fleck of glitter out and placing it in a small pouch at his waist. I had no idea what he was collecting them for. Possibly to decorate the new kazoo he'd been making for Precious's birthday, but it could also have been for the decorative inlay on one of his new guitars. He was slightly obsessed with finding uses for all the glitter.

"It's not harsh enough," Hope replied. "We can't just look away from this sort of thing. It's a serious infraction."

"Are we certain she did it on purpose?" Mikhail asked,

turning the chime over in his hand. "She can't have known—"

"I've seen Sunny's thoughts. I heard Precious's confession. And Perception just left our home. It's very, very serious, Mikhail." Hope's nostrils flared. "I can't believe you of all people would excuse her behavior, and with the Protector who was once her teacher."

All three of my mates sat up straighter and straighter as Hope spoke, like hunting dogs alerting at a scent. "*What* behavior, Hope?" Gavriel demanded, his voice a growl.

Oh, crapsickles.

Sunny stood up, rubbing her temples like she had a terrible headache. "Presh jumped Percy in the hot springs. She kissed him. He was angry. She's ashamed."

"Fuck."

Sunny winced at Gavriel's once-in-a-decade curse, and I tried to re-center our discussion. "That's not as important as what she did to the naming chime. Focus, family."

"I'll focus on unmaking him," Righteous snapped, springing into the air and flying toward the farthest edge of the Limen settlement.

Percy lived there, as far from our house as he could get, without falling off the edge into the Void. I'd wondered at his choice, but I had a terrible feeling he'd been trying to avoid this scenario, or something like it. He was Perception, after all. He might have seen this coming.

"Come back, Ry!" I yelled after him. "Gavriel, Ry doesn't understand."

Gavriel's face looked like a thunderstorm as well. "He understands enough." When I whimpered, he went on. "He won't hurt him, much. But he'll make sure Percy knows to be more aware of his surroundings in future."

"It's not Percy's fault she has a crush," I insisted, but Mikhail shook his head.

"He's known of her fixation on him, for some time. We all have. He promised me he'd make certain she knew he was not interested in her that way. I think a reminder of that promise may be overdue." He cracked his knuckles one by one.

"I swear, you're all a bunch of Neanderthals," I muttered. "Percy didn't do anything. And Precious has learned her lesson." *Sweet pickle relish, I hope so.*

Hope gave a short laugh. "The first crush I had was on a Protector named Exuberance. When they gave up their name to become a Guide, I cried for a week."

"Guides were off limits?" I asked, curious. "Or just taboo?"

"Very taboo." Hope shuddered. "But I still followed them around Sanctuary for weeks after they were in their robe and hood...until one of my friends gently let me know I was stalking the wrong Guide." She covered her face. "My cohort teased me for decades."

Sunny snorted. "The Guides did all look the same in those outfits."

I grinned. "The first time I had a crush on a guy on Earth —well, besides Righteous—I did all sorts of ridiculous things to get him to notice me."

"You, ridiculous?" Sunny teased, handing me a cup filled with steaming hot chocolate. "That's so out of character, birch."

I shot her the finger, but thanked her for the drink. "He was a farmhand, and it was harvest time. I used to hide in the wheatfields and make noises like a lost lamb to see if he would come and rescue me." I frowned, remembering. "But he never came looking. Apparently, my lamb impression sounded like some sort of monster, and they accused Laurel, the one-eyed daughter of the farmer, of being a witch and calling demons into the crop. They tied her to a stake to burn her."

"What happened?" Hope asked absently, her eyes scanning the horizon.

"Just what you'd expect. Turns out the farmhand I loved had a thing for Laurel. He came running with wet blankets and a bucket of water, but tripped and cracked his head open trying to save her. I ended up getting Laurel free." I frowned, remembering her response to my heroism. "She wasn't a witch, but she ended up being a word that rhymes with it. She threw me back into the flames. Burning alive sucks. One out of ten do not recommend."

"One out of ten?" Sunny asked curiously. "Why not zero?"

I shrugged. "It was terrible, but not as bad as the piranhas. Now *that* was a zero." I'd take burning over being eaten alive by fish any day.

"I would go back and burn down the world for you, sweet soul," Mikhail growled into my hair as he pulled me onto his lap and nuzzled my neck. "They didn't deserve you."

"None of us do," Gavriel agreed, running his hands along the tops of my wings as we waited. I closed my eyes and tried to relax.

We didn't wait long. In less than five minutes, Ry was winging back across the Limen, followed by Perception, who was flying a little less steadily.

When they landed, we all stood. I winced at the purpling around one of Percy's eyes. His red hair was long enough to pull over it if he needed to, though I was almost certain he would heal himself at one of the wells before then.

"Feather," he said, not meeting my eyes. "You have to know, I didn't mean to let her get so close. I'm... I'm sorry."

Oh, shizz. An apology? That boded extremely forking ill.

"Sorry?" My voice had a bit more snap to it than usual, and he did meet my gaze then. "Why would you need to apologize? Tell me that's not guilt in your eyes, Perception." I stepped up to him, glaring at one of the Protectors I never once would have thought capable of betraying my trust. "Tell me you didn't encourage my little girl to—"

"I would *never*. Feather, I have done everything I could to protect her feelings, and make sure she knew I wasn't interested, without hurting her." His voice was like a violin's bow scraping across an untuned string. Agonized. Raw. "But I failed. I'll... I'll have to leave."

"Where would you go?" I asked quietly, trying to keep the panic and fear out of my tone. "Where could you go, Percy?"

He glanced at Mikhail, who shook his head gently. "We won't be able to build any farther out on the Limen, Perception. Not for a long while."

"That limits my options," Perception whispered. Mikhail stared at Percy, then nodded once.

I swallowed hard, uncertain of what the two men had spoken in silence. But I trusted Mikhail more than myself, more than anyone. He would protect our daughter if it meant ending the universe for her.

Or bending it to fit her.

Perception's shoulders sagged. "You all know I tried to be her teacher. It was fine for the first few years, but after a while, I could sense her growing attraction. I swear to you all, I never encouraged it."

I relaxed slightly. "What do we do now?"

His brow furrowed. "*We* do nothing. I know what I need to do, though. To make her understand once and for all that I see her as a child."

Sunny stepped up to him. "Do you, Perception? Do you see her as a child?"

"I do." His tone was gentle, his words simple and honest. "I apologized only because I should have been more aware. She took me by surprise. I was tired." His cheeks colored. "I wasn't paying attention. Honestly, I think she slipped and fell into the hot spring. She seemed as shocked as I was to... be in that situation."

Sunny grimaced. "But she took advantage."

Percy nodded grimly. "She'll apologize to you," I started, but he cut me off.

"No. She needs to keep her distance. I'll make it clear to everyone that I'm not available."

I narrowed my eyes. "*How* will you do that?" I asked, but I already knew.

His chin jutted out. "I'll merge with someone. A Protector. I'll... I'll take a mate, if I must."

The realm around us went silent, our shocked gasps all that interrupted the tense moment.

It was Righteous who broke the pall. "Bind yourself eternally to another soul, just to make a point? That's the stupidest thing I've ever heard you say, Percy. Let's go get a drink." He dropped a kiss on my head, then grabbed Percy. They'd already flown away before any of the rest of us could react.

"What was that about?" Sunny asked, her eyes narrowing with suspicion.

Mikhail hummed under his breath, then spoke slowly, as if he was carefully choosing each word. "Righteous has lived through a somewhat similar experience, I believe. Unwanted attention. When my sweet soul assaulted him in Sanctuary?"

I sputtered, then blew a raspberry, remembering how I'd kissed Ry when he'd been a basshole to Sunny. And me. And everyone. I had almost ruined his life, and ended up almost dying when he couldn't be purified. "Yeah, I guess I see where she gets it from."

Sunny nudged me with her foot. "To be fair, Ry deserved all that smut you covered him with. He was a real jerk."

"I still shouldn't have kissed him without his consent," I mumbled.

Mikhail made a thoughtful sound. "A very similar story. Though Righteous's ended happily."

I couldn't see how this story could possibly end well, though. Precious had driven Perception to the end of his rope, and I wasn't certain if she understood how badly she'd botched things up.

Hope groaned, burying her face in her hands. "I think I need a drink."

"I *know* we do," Sunny and I said at the same time.

CHAPTER 6
Righteous

I led Perception back to the new Merge and spoke a word of power at the main door, locking it behind us. Not that anyone would come in; the building was off limits until the next night, when the opening ceremony—and supposedly the naming—would take place. The entire realm was at home today, preparing food, drinks, and risqué costumes for the big event.

I stepped behind the bar, grabbing two golden cups and a small keg of beer that Mikhail had made the week before, back when we were working on the furniture. I handed a cup to Perception, who nodded and sat on a bench, but kept his distance. As if he didn't trust me not to hit him again.

"I shouldn't have punched you," I admitted, ashamed of my earlier knee-jerk reaction. Perception was one of my closest friends, and I knew him. He was honorable, a decent man down to his bedrock foundation. "I overreacted. I'm so sorry, Percy."

"No," he said, rubbing his face with a hand. "I should have apologized, rather than tell you to merge with a cactus." It was all I could do not to punch him again when he added, "I'm ashamed of myself. Of what happened with your daughter."

My hands tightened into fists again, just in case I needed to give him a matching black eye. "Why would you be?"

He glanced up, eyes wild. "No, no! Not for that... Listen, it had been a long day. Adoration had been asking for extra help with Earth history lessons, and Precious had somehow snuck away from Tradition, or finished her lessons early. I'm not sure. She'd been hanging around, leaving glitter all over my office, glaring at Adoration."

"Did she glare hard enough to burn holes in her?" I asked, joking.

"A couple," he replied, not joking at all.

Oh shit. I'd need to tell the others to keep Adoration far, far away from Precious for the next few years. Maybe decades. Until she was done with her adolescence.

Percy dropped his gaze to the floor. "I was exhausted at the end of the day. I went to the hot springs, and I wasn't paying attention." He laughed humorlessly. "Perception is literally who I am, but I didn't perceive her presence."

"She's good at being quiet when she wants to be. Sneaky, like her mom."

"True. I was meditating in the pool and drifted off, dreaming. In my dream, I'd found my soulmate."

"Who?" I asked, wildly curious. Dreams could be portents. Prophecies. More than one Protector had dreamed of their mate here in the Limen, and bonded.

"I couldn't see her. She shone so bright, though. Made of light, her body almost faceted like a gem. She had her arms around me, her lips on mine. And before I was awake, before I knew what was happening, it was real—but it wasn't her. It was Precious." He went silent.

"Perception?" I moved closer as he shuddered. His eyes

were brimming. "How long have you been dreaming of your soulmate, friend?"

"Since we left Sanctuary." His red-rimmed eyes met mine, his words rumbling over each other as he tried to explain. "But I haven't found her. No one, not even Seraphiel, shines like the woman in my dreams."

"Don't give up," I said earnestly. "Don't mate with someone else just to protect yourself. We'll do better. We'll keep her away—" His harsh laughter cut me off.

"How? If I move any farther away, my house will fall into the void. I've spoken with Imriel about somehow getting a Celestial key and going to Earth on a mission."

"You don't have to leave, Percy."

"What else can I do? This realm is so small. I can't read her mind; none of us can. She's always there, trying to get my attention. In good and bad ways." A rueful smile flickered, then died. "She acts tough, but her heart is so tender. So I've tried to be subtle. Tried not to embarrass her." His jaw tightened as if he were in pain. "Do I need to be cruel? Is that it?"

"I don't recommend it. When I met Feather, I was beyond cruel to her. I was monstrous. And my shame manifested itself on my skin." I winced, remembering how I'd stewed in my rage until I was almost as dirty as she had been. "I looked like I'd been wrestling pigs."

"You smelled every bit as bad."

"You don't stink, Percy. And you're as clean as you've ever been. You haven't done anything wrong. Don't start now. We'll find a way to keep her away."

He snorted. "A gate? You'll need a *great* one."

I punched his arm just hard enough to spill his beer a little. "Too soon, Percy." We drank in silence for a moment. "If Mik still had a working naming chime, I'm sure he'd use it to build you a Precious-proof security system. He'd probably welcome the challenge."

Perception blanched. "The chime is broken?" Quickly, I explained what had happened. When I was done, he cursed aloud. "Nothing is safe from her these days, is it? She's a Celestial wrecking ball."

"Harsh." I rose to take our empty cups to the kitchen near the back door. "I know you didn't mean that, so I'll forgive you this time. But don't talk about her like that again."

A shadow moved across the half-open back doorway, and I cursed myself for not checking that entrance. I peered outside, seeing only a few Protectors seated around a picnic table a few hundred feet away. I reached out with my thoughts to check for any other Protectors, but the area was clear. At least, *now* it was.

I sent a question to Seraphiel. *Are you with Precious?*

Yes, he replied immediately. I let out a sigh of relief and returned to Percy, who was already halfway through another mug of beer. I was surprised; he normally didn't like to have his thoughts clouded, though I supposed today's events would be better seen through a beer-haze.

I rested a hand on his slumped shoulder. "You know, none of us knew Precious's infatuation had gone this far. You could have asked for help."

"I asked Seraphiel. He had me turn her classes over to the lower-level Guides the first time I noticed her flirting with me two years ago." He laughed, a desperate sound that was somehow also filled with pride. "Righteous, she's a savant. She learned everything they had to teach—what should have taken a decade—in two years. I ended up giving her instructors the hardest exams I could dream up, just so she'd have something to keep her engaged. The Guides who filled in for me all loved working with her, at first. But she broke them in the process with her insubordinate questions, her filthy language, her antics."

"Antics? She burned down the school on purpose."

"Ah, you figured that out?"

I snorted. "You covered it up?"

He took a long gulp of beer. "I didn't want Tradition to stop teaching her. He's the only one with close to the breadth of knowledge to be her teacher now. Many days, even he can't answer her questions."

"What about Gavriel?"

"We tried that. He goes too easy on her," he protested. "Same with Seraphiel."

"Maybe she doesn't need as much time in the classroom," I began. "She could work at the energy wells—"

"Absolutely not, Ry. She needs to know as much as possible before—" His jaw clicked shut.

"Before what?" I asked.

Percy shook his head once. "I promised Imriel I would keep this secret."

I knew he and Imriel shared almost everything. Since we'd arrived in the Limen, Percy had been flying to the closed gate between this realm and the Celestial one, singing through the ugly fire door. Sharing knowledge, and building a friendship. But it had become clear long ago that what the two focused on most days was Precious. Her education, though most of her lessons with the eldest Guide, Tradition, were centered around ethics and morality, not mathematics and literature.

Seraphiel was in on the secret meetings, too. He still had visions of the future, and after he'd had one about Precious the year before, I'd found him weeping over her as she slept. But when I'd asked him to share, he'd said that saying some things aloud made them more possible. More real.

And if the future he and Perception feared awaited our little girl was enough to put terror in the eyes of the oldest of all of us? I knew better than to pry.

"Righteous," Percy said softly, his too-wise eyes meeting mine. "Even if I can't stay in the Limen... the rest of you can never give up on teaching her how to be as good as she can be. As much of a *Protector* as possible."

The implication of his words chilled me. I remembered the horrified faces of the Celestials when we'd first entered that realm. Her smut, her glitter, and her horns had the eternal beings there frightened. There had been mutterings about prophecies and the ending of the realm. But I couldn't believe the Precious we all knew and loved could be capable of destroying the universe. Though she did enjoy fire a little too much for anyone's comfort.

As Feather would say, it was definitely time to change the subject. "You know what? I'm hungry. Let's fly over to the Limenteria and grab some food. Maybe I can swing a few votes to my name for this place while we're there. I was thinking The Pulse of Pleasure. But now I'm leaning toward The Glory Spot." I grinned, and was relieved when he smiled back.

"The G Spot? Righteous, I think your little mate has worn off on you. Your names are getting worse every time."

"Or are they getting better?" I mused aloud, and Perception laughed.

Mission accomplished.

CHAPTER 7
Seraphiel

I found Precious at the darkest edge of the Limen, staring into the void, and landed, lowering myself to sit beside her. In the distance, her dog raced across the cloud floor, stirring up puffs of glitter, stopping every so often to alert at the void, as if he saw or heard something there.

I didn't like to think about what might be out here, watching my little girl.

Tempting her.

The void had a way of slithering into your mind and whispering suggestions. Convincing you that right was wrong. That imbalance was balance. That there was no hope, or light, or peace to be found, and destruction was the answer to the pain of existence.

I would know about its tricks; I'd spent a vast portion of my nearly eternal life lost in the void. Listening to its lies. Trying to redeem the souls that had gotten mired there. I ran a hand over my arm, feeling the nearly invisible traces of where I'd carried them for so long, the lines they had carved into my soul that I had kept, even after I'd been transformed in the

Celestial Realm. I'd kept them so I'd always remember the task of saving them was incomplete.

"Something you want to talk about, Little Glitter?"

"They found it, didn't they?" she said after a long moment. "Is Dad..." Her voice broke off as she tried to ask about Mikhail. I wrapped my arms around her, holding her on my lap while she sobbed. I was the only one of her parents who could see into her thoughts, though even for me it was like listening to whispers from miles away.

....*He'll hate me... evil... knew better... didn't even work... I'm a devil... twisted...*

"You're not twisted," I said gently. "You're not evil. You're perfect. Stop thinking of the parts of your name that you think are bad, and see the whole."

"Perfect *Devil*, Baba." She wiped her face with the back of her arm. Her eyes were bleak, the swirling galaxies in them dimmed, when she finally dragged her gaze to mine. "I'm not like any of the others here. Not like you. I'm evil. I want to do bad things."

"We've talked about this. You have choices, my perfect Little Glitter. All you must do is learn everything you can, and then try to make the ones you can live with."

Her lips quivered. "I was trying to choose. I wanted to choose a new name, one that would mean I wasn't... like this."

"That you weren't you?" My own voice broke. "Oh, my sweet girl, I would never want to live in a universe that didn't have you in it, just as you are. My perfect child, my beloved daughter." I pressed my lips to her silky, dark purple hair.

"The others think I'm going to bring about the end of the universe, Baba. They whisper about it when they think I can't hear."

I sighed heavily. "I've tried to tell them most of those old prophecies were made up when I was drunk off my ass. Glitter

49

will bring the end of the realm? The shadow will fall over every Celestial and silence the Eternal Hymn, blah blah blah. You know I was mostly punking them." Or at least, I had thought I was.

She snorted a tiny laugh. "Well, I wish your *fake* prophecies didn't line up quite so neatly with my *real* existence, Baba."

I kissed her head again, giving her a squeeze, before moving away an inch and changing the subject. "Make me a marshmallow?" She held out a hand and focused on it, only screwing up her nose a tiny bit to make the fluffiest marshmallow I'd ever seen appear. It was perfectly golden brown, just as I preferred them. "Thank you, Little Glitter."

A mournful howl sounded in the distance, followed by the thump of racing paws as Shadow smelled his favorite treat. Laughing, Precious created a new one and half-incinerated it before tossing it over her shoulder. Shadow gobbled it up, gave a woof of thanks, then went back to prowling the cloud edge, growling at the glittering void.

"Shadow does that a lot these days," I said absently, observing Precious's face as she narrowed her eyes at the same patch of darkness. "Keeping watch. Any idea what he sees?"

"What could possibly be out there?" she replied, a non-answer if I'd ever heard one. She could lie to most of the others. But not to me.

"You know what's out there, don't you? Precious, you have to know the void isn't your friend." She had insisted when she was little that the void was alive. That it talked to her and played with her. That it was lonely. I'd caught her a dozen times trying to fly off into it to meet the imaginary friend she called Void Boy.

"You've told me that a thousand times." Another non-answer. She made a huffing sound, materialized another marshmallow, and stuffed it into her mouth.

Shadow and I shared a long look. I wished again that the

Singer of All Songs had given the temple dogs the power to speak. They held so much of the universe's deepest truths in their spiritual forms...

I sighed as Precious nudged me with an elbow. "Stop staring. You'll make him self-conscious," she teased.

"The void isn't a person," I reminded her again. "It has no conscience. It is a total lack of all spirit and life."

She leaned up against me, examining my nails. They were sharper than anyone's except her own, though hers were deep purple and glittery, while mine glowed with golden Celestial fire. "It's not a total lack. Earth is out there. Will you tell me about it?"

"What do you want to know this time? Aren't you tired of hearing about Earth?" I asked, closing my eyes as my daughter stared at my golden horns and tail, as she often did. She and I were the only ones with horns in the Limen, though hers were a deep charcoal. And only I had a tail, a souvenir from my eons of imprisonment in the Abyss.

"You never talk about it unless I ask." Precious tossed bits of burned marshmallows out into the void. "And it's not boring like Earth history class." She hesitated a moment, and I sensed there was something in particular she wanted to ask. "How long were you alive? Did you... Did you have a family there? Kids, a daughter like me?"

I could feel her underlying fear, and though she had her mental connection shut down entirely, I heard her question: *A real daughter?*

"You are my real daughter," I said gently. "You've even got my horns."

She shot me an impatient glare. "But did you? Did you have a wife or husband, or a lover?"

"No, I didn't," I replied, pondering how much to share with her. "I didn't even kiss anyone. Well, not romantically."

"How?" she asked, dumbfounded. "How could you

possibly live on Earth for all those years, and not do one thing wrong? I told four lies before breakfast this morning. I yelled at Mom and Tata Sunny and Mama Hope like twelve times this week."

"That's not so bad," I drawled. "Your recent behavior could be called an improvement on last year when you *burned down your school*."

She sighed, defeated. "Really? What if I told you I tried to kill a Protector this week?"

I blinked. "Did you really?"

She shrugged. "I kicked Adoration when she was leaning over at the well, gathering energy. She got hurt trying to get free; she almost drowned. And I was glad. I *wanted* to hurt her, Baba. I liked it." Her spirit seemed to crumple in on itself, like a piece of tinfoil. "I'm not good like everyone else here. Sometimes I feel it inside my body, like the Limen is a magnet and so am I, but our poles are facing each other. I'm being pushed away. I don't belong."

I didn't react, but only because I'd had years of practice hiding my pain. I knew her journey was going to take her far away from us. But I would do everything in my power to keep her here as long as possible. To protect her as well as I could. "You do. I promise you belong with the ones who love you. You have so much good in you."

She shrugged. "You have to say that—you're my dad. But I know I could never live a blameless life like you did."

I closed my eyes and sent a prayer up to the Mother of All, hoping I would say the right thing. I was about to admit something I'd only shared openly with my small soulmate.

"I couldn't either. I cheated."

Shadow woofed a few times in a row, a sound so close to laughter that I smiled.

Precious was staring lasers into my face now. "No. Way."

"Yes way," I replied, fighting a laugh of my own. "I didn't

spend all that time in the Abyss without picking up a few tricks, you know. There are always loopholes, my perfect devil. And when I leaped off the roof of Sanctuary, I went right through a rather large one."

I closed my eyes, remembering, and told the story. "I was falling from the rooftop of Sanctuary, feeling it die behind me —it was terrifying. I was so scared, alone. I was supposed to become nothing but spirit. I wasn't meant to have any... direction. But I'd been alive for so long, I kept hold of my center for longer than I thought possible. I knew as I fell, even after the journey to Earth had stripped away my individual memories... I understood that there was something I needed to get back to as fast as I could."

Precious quivered with curiosity as she listened. I had never shared this with her. I didn't want her to think of me as a cheater. But today, learning that she held herself to some impossible standard, I realized it was past time for her to see that her parents were faulty, and broken, just like she saw herself.

"Every Protector is born the first time as a human. But I made certain when I directed my soul into an unborn physical form, that I would not live a normal span of years."

"What?"

I ducked my head. "In my final moments of... awareness, when I still had the smallest hint of my powers, I saw a wealthy family who had everything they wanted, except empathy. They couldn't feel for those less well off. For those who struggled. I made certain that changed.

"When I was born, I was the child they had always wanted. But as I grew, so did the terrible, life-threatening disease inside my form. My bones broke with almost every movement I made. A coughing fit would shatter ribs. It was a painful, short life I lived. But I was loved." My heart ached, remembering. "So loved. They poured their lives into trying to save me, and others like me. When I was dying, my parents established a foundation, called Raphael's Respite. It provided free lodging for any parents in North America who needed to stay near a hospital and didn't have the funds."

Her jaw had dropped wide, and I shut it with one finger. "Baba, that would have shifted the balance a lot... right?"

"I would hope so. Without Protectors on Earth now to help the balance, they'll need all the help they can get."

"But couldn't it spoil the balance instead, that you cheated to make it happen?"

That question had haunted me for years now. I shrugged. "I made the choice, and I can't change it now. Am I glad things worked out as they did, that I was able to return to your mother, you, our family?" I stared directly into her face and told a terrible truth. "I would have sacrificed almost anything to be where I am right now, with the ones I love most. Even the balance of all the realms."

Her eyes gleamed with what could have been approval or censure. "So the end justified the means?"

"I like to think I was only fudging the rules, Little Glitter. Not burning them all down."

"Fixing them." The galaxies in her eyes began whirling faster, like they did when she had an idea, but she didn't speak, only smiled at the void. I met Shadow's gaze and thought I saw a matching worry there.

Speaking of fixing things... "What were you trying to change your name to?" I asked gently.

"Who even cares? It didn't work. And now I'll be grounded for a year."

"Possibly much longer." I stood, holding out a hand. "I think your dad was muttering something about you turning two hundred. You need to apologize to him. And to Perception." Though I had a feeling he wouldn't want to get close enough for her to do that in person. Maybe a letter would suffice.

Her cheeks darkened with a blush as she wrapped her wings tightly around herself. "Did Mom tell you? Or Tata Sunny?"

"No."

"Then who?"

"Does it matter?"

Her shoulders slumped, and flecks of deep lavender glitter sloughed off her wings and onto the clouds below. "I guess not."

The hardest part of being a parent was not being able to soothe every hurt, to bend the world to fit your child's dreams. But the sort of change she'd been trying for wasn't possible, and even the attempt came at much too high a cost. Some consequences could not be avoided.

Something in my heart told me that Precious was going to learn that lesson soon.

CHAPTER 8
Feather

My oldest mate was easy to find in the sky over the Limen. Rumple glowed, his vast wings and bright skin every bit as polished as they had been when he emerged from the Celestial Realm and came back to me in the Limen. The matching golden horns and tail were every bit as shiny, and I sent a kiss to him down our soul bond. The feather he'd wrapped around my left breast gave a warm, reassuring throb.

Precious wasn't as easy to spot, but she was there, flying a few hundred feet behind. Her deeper coloration was almost a match for the glittering void behind her.

"The Abyss doesn't have glitter," I mused aloud from my seat on the soft grass. "Not from what Rumple told me."

Gavriel fed another grape in between my lips, and I leaned back into his arms. I wished we could run back to our bedroom, lock the door, and open another 55-gallon drum of lube. Or at least another jar of maple syrup. I was not looking forward to the next few moments.

"I don't believe it did. The void didn't either, not all that long ago. But the glitter you brought here from Sanctuary— and the glitter Mikhail created for you—is spreading into the void around us. It's changing." Gavriel's voice was filled with wonder, and amusement. Maybe a little concern. "Each piece reflects any available light, of course. But from what Rumple, Mikhail, and I have figured out, each speck of this glitter has a balancing property. Which is odd. Glitter is, by its very nature, a tool for great evil."

I punched him lightly in the side. "Glitter is not inherently evil."

"Agree to disagree, my love." He hummed an apology against the top of my head, his clever hands moving over my ribs and sides like I was a living xylophone. "But we do believe glitter, even if it is a force for ill, can be used as a tool by the Maker of All to spread light in the darkest places. Perhaps it's already doing so."

It wasn't the first time one of my mates had mused about this, but Gavriel was the most circumspect of all of us. If he had come to this conclusion, it was almost a certainty.

I pushed his fingers away from my neck, where he was messing with Mikhail's mating feather. "Stop teasing me, Gav. The glitter is rebalancing the void around us—is that what you're telling me?"

"Not just a pretty face, are you?"

I smiled smugly over my shoulder. "So glitter is saving the universe, not destroying it. You've been wrong all this time. Glitter is *good*. Holy, even."

"I wouldn't go that far," he said with a laugh and a tickle that made me squirm and almost pee a little. I went to punch him again, but he picked me up. I settled for wrapping my legs around him as he unfurled his wings of light around us.

"So shiny," I whispered, half-entranced as usual by the glow that surrounded us. When I'd first met my mates, I'd thought being dickmatized was the thing. I'd never realized how hot *wings* were. Especially wings that had as many divine nerve endings as these. I ran my finger along one edge of the light, and Gavriel growled.

"Not now, little wretch. We have to be the bad guys."

"I hate being the bad guys."

"All good parents do."

In less than a minute, Presh and Rumple landed. Gavriel and I stood, waiting under the golden aspen trees in the park. Rumple blew me a kiss and walked away, leaving the three of us to take seats on the sturdy benches, with Presh on the smallest one.

She'd added all sorts of marks into it over the years, carving them with her sharp nails. I hadn't realized until just now that I'd seen marks like those before. Not the angelic sigils that made up our written language, but demonic ones. She'd used a mixture of demonic and baby-babble for the first years of her life, but it had been a long time since I'd heard her speak it. Most of the Protectors and Guides here said it hurt their ears to hear it. One of the younger residents had bled from the ears when she'd thrown a tantrum, shouting in demonic.

Did she still speak it when she was alone? Did she still remember it?

A thought came to mind. "Presh," I said in a whisper. "When you talk to the void, what language do you speak in?"

She didn't answer, but her eyes went wide, and her cheeks flushed a deeper purple.

"Never mind," I murmured as Mikhail walked out of our house. I had my answer.

"Dad, I can explain about the chime," Precious said, standing when he approached with the golden chime in his hand. We had all agreed we wouldn't talk about the Perception problem in a group. A girl's—no, a young woman's first kiss should not be the subject of a family meeting.

Mikhail didn't smile, but his deep bass voice rumbled with acceptance. "You don't need to explain what happened. I already know, and my shiny, lovely, stubborn girl? I already forgave you. You never even have to ask."

Precious burst into tears and raced to him, burying her face in the glittery shirt that covered his broad chest. It was all I could do not to cry along with her as she hiccupped through a dozen more apologies. Finally, we all sat back down, Presh next to Mikhail, her eyes stuck on the ruined chime in his open palm.

"You don't need to explain," Mikhail said again, infinite patience in his expression. "I know what it is to be young, and in love with the idea of being something else. Someone else. I know you tried to change your name."

She nodded. "I d-didn't know I could hurt it, Dad. I thought it would just... work, or not work. That's what you said before. That it was unbreakable."

Mikhail paused for a moment. "I thought it was. I was wrong."

"I ruin *everything*," Precious whispered at her lap. "I'm a disaster."

"No, little spark. You are not a disaster. You're a force to be reckoned with. So powerful in ways you did not realize. But to be fair, neither did we." Presh looked up, confused. "The chime would have remained intact, even when used inappropriately as you did, for anyone else. Well, anyone other than you, or perhaps me or your mom." He nodded to me, and I chewed at my lip, uncertain of where he was going with this. "Feather and I are both Namers. I became one through centuries upon centuries of training, and then your mom became one when I gave her my mating feather."

We were all silent, before Presh spoke again. "You mean, I'm a Namer, too? I'm like you?" She blinked furiously. "I broke it because I'm... powerful?"

"I believe so. And that is why the consequences of your actions will include your assistance in repairing the chime." *If it can be fixed*, he sent to me. *I would not wager that it can be repaired at all.*

I understood immediately. *But she needs to try.*

She must. From the way it's been deformed, only her mixture of power has any hope of restoring it. And only the attempt can bring balance to her actions.

"Every day, instead of going to school, you'll report to my workshop," Mikhail pronounced, his tone stern. "You will be my apprentice, and not my child, in that space. You will do everything I ask of you without question. You will not be allowed to socialize, or even sleep unless your duties are done each day. And your duties will be comprehensive."

Precious swallowed hard at the unyielding steel in her father's voice. Other than Righteous, Mikhail was the biggest softie of the bunch. But I had a feeling that was about to change.

It will keep her away from Perception as well, Gavriel thought. *By the time she's completed her apprenticeship, she won't even remember he exists.*

"How long is an apprenticeship?" I squeaked out loud. Precious nodded quickly, like she'd been thinking the same thing.

Mikhail closed his hand around the chime. "Mine was eight hundred years, give or take. But Precious is a clever girl. I can't imagine it would take her any longer than that. Maybe only seven hundred." He turned away from the rest of us, but not before I saw the sly wink he sent my direction.

Presh didn't see it. She started to sputter and fume, but Gavriel stood up, with one hand raised. "Those are the consequences for breaking the chime. Stay quiet. You have more coming your way for stealing it, and using Shadow to hide your crime."

As if he'd heard his name, Shadow came galloping into the

park, skidding to a stop as he took in all our faces. He slunk to Precious's side.

"Shadow will not be allowed to sleep in your room for the foreseeable future," Gavriel finished, with an apologetic nod to the dog.

"What?" Precious's wings bristled, and dark glitter filled the air around her as she beat them furiously. "Why would you punish him?"

Gavriel didn't blink. "You used his bedding to conceal what you'd done. For all we know, he assisted you intentionally. So his bed will no longer be in your private space. He may sleep in the hallway or outside the house." She burst into tears, kneeling to embrace Shadow. Gavriel's features might as well have been made of marble for all the emotion he showed her. "The punishment is yours, and fits the crime. I'm disappointed that you would include him in your mistake. If you'd come to us immediately, only you would have been held accountable." He dropped his gaze to the dog. "I'm sorry, Shadow."

I'd never heard a dog cry before, and I never wanted to hear it again.

"I hate you," Precious hissed as she held her dog and cried into his charcoal gray fur. "I hate all of you."

Not for the first time, I wished that I could hear whether my daughter was lying or not. I wanted to think she was just lashing out.

But it sounded like the truth.

Gavriel gave a heavy sigh, dropped a kiss on my head, and walked quietly away, toward his music room. Mikhail came over for a longer hug and whispered in my ear, "Talk to her?" *And then send her to my workshop*, he thought. *We need to keep her busy, so her anger won't fester.*

I knew what he meant. When Precious got mad, it didn't fade over time. It seemed to grow, like a forest fire, until she was totally out of control, doing and saying things she couldn't take back.

I sat close to Precious on the ground, not touching her. After a few minutes of weeping, Shadow moved closer to me so I could pat him, and I marveled at the soft strands of his Celestial fur, as always. "Softer than my sheets," I murmured. "Even if you're a whole lot dirtier."

"He's not bad. He's not dirty. It's not his fault," Presh rasped.

She might have meant the dark gray of his coat, or the chime; I wasn't sure. But I didn't look at her, or stop patting. I just gave her my own truth. "I know. It was my color for a long time. When I was in Sanctuary, I was covered in smut. And just like this dog, none of it meant I was bad. Most of it wasn't even mine."

"But you killed people. Like, a lot of them, right?"

I patted Shadow a little faster. "Sure, but not innocent people. And if I could do it any other way, if I could protect the vulnerable people I had to, I didn't murder."

She scoffed. "I've heard the stories."

I looked up into her reddened, disbelieving eyes. "I'm not lying. I mean, sure, maybe I could have found slightly less violent ways of helping rebalance the Earth. But I didn't know what I was doing. I made mistakes. I messed things up." I grabbed her hand. "And I was still deserving of love. Your dads fell in love with me, mated with me, when I was a whole lot dirtier than Shadow here. And I had done a lot worse things than you could dream."

She whispered, "I remember killing the bad guys on Earth, sometimes."

I sucked in a breath. I'd wondered. She'd only been a toddler, but she had been like a miniature, fuzzy-winged Genghis Khan, rolling over the continents on Earth for those few months, instinctively finding the worst pedophiles, murderers, and rapists, the most corrupt politicians, and slaughtering them with all the joy of a preschooler knocking down sandcastles.

"I was happy when I killed them. It felt good." She pulled her hand away and held it up, both of us staring at the smears of charcoal and deep purple that lay under the surface. The glittery stain of her crimes had soaked into her very being. "I wish it didn't mean that everyone could see how bad I am, all the time. That's all I wanted, with the chime, you know. To be purified like the rest of you."

My heart broke into glitter-sized pieces as she went on. "Do you know how hard it is to be the daughter of the greatest heroes of the universe? To have a Great Sacrifice for a mom? To look in the mirror every morning and know I'll never be able to be like you?" She hiccupped softly. "I wanted to be worthy. To measure up to you, Mom."

I knew she hated to be hugged, most of the time. But I couldn't do anything else. I took her into my arms and squeezed her as I answered, as if I could force the truth of my words into her very bones. "Precious, my glitter baby, my beloved child, you *more* than measure up. You're the center of my universe, the beating heart inside my chest. Never think that you are less than me, or anyone. You. Are. Perfect." I infused those words with all the truth I could. She gasped in my embrace, then relaxed.

When I pulled away, we had matching tearful expressions. "What did you try to change your name to, baby? If you don't want me to tell anyone else, I won't. But tell me."

"I only tried to add a few words," she murmured. "After the first part—Precious, Perfect Devil, Little Glitter, shiny, and lovely, and stubborn—I tried to add 'and pure.'"

I blinked. "You tried to purify yourself with the chime? That's all?" There was no way that would have melted the chime. In fact, it might have worked, though it could have unmade her as it purified her.

"That's all." Her left eye twitched.

"Try again, hon."

She covered her face with her hand, so I almost didn't hear the next words. "I also added 'and Infinitely Seductive and Irresistibly Sexy.' And I might have tacked on something about having 'Bounteous Boobs Beyond a B Cup.'"

I bit the inside of my cheek so hard, trying not to laugh. I was surprised my teeth didn't bite through.

"Don't say anything," she muttered, but when her hands descended, I noticed her mouth twitching. I mimed zipping my lips. After a second, she rolled her eyes. "Go ahead, say it."

I grinned at her, pushing a few strands of her glittering hair away from her face and cupping her sharp chin in my hands. "We may not look alike on the outside, but no one can ever say you didn't inherit my Naming skills."

"And your lack of boobs," she groaned.

"Yeah." I sighed, looking down at Agnes and Esther, who poked out like two chocolate kisses hiding under my toga top. "And that."

CHAPTER 9
Feather
THREE WEEKS LATER

"Sunny, are you sure this costume isn't too high cut?" I turned to peer at my back in the mirror. "I think you can see my underwear."

"When did you start wearing underwear, birch?" Sunny snarked.

I didn't answer. This was a special pair I'd glitter painted especially for Growly, which said *Spank Here*. He probably wouldn't. Even after years of hinting that he didn't have to be quite so gentle in bed, he was still reluctant to do anything that even reminded him of when I was hurt. Or that I could get hurt. Or, even worse, that he might hurt me.

"Rough play is more Seraphiel's or Gavriel's thing, isn't it, sweet soul?" he'd said only the night before. But he would never be able to resist a hand-painted invitation on my caboose, not on opening night in The Merge Two.

"The Merge Two: Electric Boogaloo," I hummed as I took a breath so my boobs would poke out a bit more.

"That's not going to be what wins," Sunny interrupted. "No one but you would vote for that."

I stuck out my tongue. Every resident of the Limen, except

for Shadow and Precious, had cast anonymous votes for the name of the new sex club, and tonight, Rumple would announce the winner at the costume party. Then Mikhail would use the somewhat-repaired naming chime to finish the sign. And then we'd all have group sex in the big room.

Well, everyone but me and my guys. None of them wanted anyone else to see me naked, even though I'd been kind of curious about what an entire realm having an orgy would look like, so they'd decided to drink, dance, and dip early. We'd already set up the chocolate fountain and the most vital macramé creations in our bedroom to make sure our private mini-orgy was a sexual smorgasbord to remember.

"What did you vote for?" I asked Sunny as she slipped on her tall, golden, gladiator sandals. She was going as Queen Midas, and she was gold all over, with streaks of her gorgeous dark skin peeking through the paint.

I had a pair of shimmery silver tennis shoes to go with my own tiny nurse costume, and a silver stethoscope around my neck. My hair was up in pigtails on both sides of my face, with a cute nurse's cap on top. *Hmm.* I peeked at my reflection. It still needed something.

"Freckles!" I ran through to the bedroom and grabbed one of our jars of chocolate sauce, then used my eyeliner brush to dab a few cute freckles on my cheeks.

"Holy sheet, birch, you look like every dirty old man's wettest dream," Sunny said with a low whistle when I turned.

I sniffed. "I should hope so. I'm married to some of the oldest men in existence."

"And some of the dirtiest, too," she teased, linking arms as we stepped outside. "On the inside, at least. And that's what counts." Laughing, we began the short walk to the party. I glanced back at our house, slightly worried, though I knew I didn't have a real reason to be.

Shadow had agreed to stand guard outside Precious's

bedroom door to make sure she stayed grounded, though she hadn't seemed that bothered. Mikhail's punishment had given her something none of us had realized she needed: a purpose. For the past three weeks, she'd spent every waking hour in his workshop, learning everything she could about the arts of Naming and Making.

He'd confided that she had actually been the one to help repair the chime. They'd used it on a few things, and the results had been unpredictable, but generally good. Mikhail had finally admitted that, even if it wasn't perfect, using it to help make the sign for the sex club wasn't that big a deal. How wrong could it go?

A shiver went down my spine as I thought about how wrong things had gone for me, back in the day. I sent up a little prayer to the Goddess of Glittery Goofups that any stumbles tonight would be minor.

The club was heaving when we arrived. "Hope!" Sunny shouted, dropping my arm and running to join her mate on the dance floor that had gold and silver lights flashing in the floor panels. The music that poured out of the walls themselves had a deep, thumping bass line that I could feel all the way up in my hoohah.

"Did you just think of sweet Bitsy as your *hoohah*?" Righteous asked behind me, as he leaned in to kiss my neck on one side and tweak his mating feather through my toga on the other. "Nurse Feather, I think you need to check my vitals." I wanted to melt into him, but I spun around instead to see what he had on, since we'd all decided to surprise each other at the party.

"Anaconda... Pants?" I gasped as I realized that Ry was wearing green and brown body paint instead of clothing—well, he had on a schlong-thong—which made him appear to be half man, half python. I stared at the ridiculous bulge that was growing slightly more pronounced under my gaze. "It's perfect, Ry. You're the anaconda of my dreams."

Before I could grab him to see just how much bigger the tip of his "snake tail" could grow, someone threw a rope around me, like a lasso. "Hold up there, pardner," Rumple crooned in a silly Texas drawl. "Darn good thing I brought my lasso. If you cowpokes ask me, this little filly needs to be broken."

"Or ridden," I suggested, as I took in his cowboy hat, leather vest, and deputy sheriff star. My eyes dropped to the lasso, and I laughed when I realized it was his tail. Then I gasped. "Rumple, are those... are those..." I stuttered as I took in what he had on the bottom half of his gorgeous body.

He turned around, winked over his shoulder, and slapped one bare butt cheek at me. "Yes indeedy, little lady. Assless chaps for my sweet Texas rose."

"Yeehaw!" I grabbed the end of his tail from around my waist and stuck the tip in my mouth, giving it a good, thorough suck. Rumple laughed, adjusting the front of his trousers.

"Naughty girl," Gavriel purred beside me, as the rest of my mates joined us. Then he purred for real, lifted a hand to his whiskered face, and licked at it, like a paw.

My jaw dropped as I took a step back. He wore a costume that wouldn't have been out of place in the old Broadway show called *Cats*. Fur from top to bottom, with golden eyes that were distinctly catlike as he gave a soft "meow."

I hadn't been this shocked—in a good way—since Righteous had won a game of cards and made the other guys pay up by calling him Sir for a week and doing whatever he commanded. My youngest lover's stern side had spawned a whole lot of new fantasies in my already twisted mind.

Apparently, it was Gav's time to shine. As he turned, I noted the long cat's tail that descended from a slit in his tight, furry pants had to be connected directly to his... *Oh. My. Plug.*

Or to be technical, *his* plug.

"Gavriel, I thought you said you didn't have a furry kink?"

My heart pounded double time when he grinned. Gavriel was my most serious mate, and his smiles were like rainbows that lit up my entire soul. "I don't. I told you, I have a Feather kink." He wrapped a hand around the back of my neck, his fingers landing over Mikhail's mating feather as he pulled me in for a kiss.

At the last moment instead of kissing me, he licked a long stripe up the side of my face. "Meow."

"Ew!" I yelled, feigning disgust. After all, this man had licked every place his tongue could reach. Before I could retaliate, I was snatched away and tucked under Mikhail's arm. "What... Growly? Where are we going?"

He was carrying me across the dance floor, and I only had a moment to notice the kilt he was wearing, complete with kilt socks, the naming chime stuck in the top of one of them in place of the *sgian dubh* knife. I grinned. He knew how much I loved it when he read Robert Burns to me in his Scottish burr.

I slid a finger up his thigh under the kilt, just to check and see if he'd gone fully traditional. He had, but we were moving too fast for me to do anything about it.

Dancing Protectors, their faces splashed with the Celestial lights, moved out of the way as he marched through the throng. Everyone was having an amazing time. Which meant no one was paying attention to us. That was a good thing, considering my nurse costume had slipped up, leaving my glittery underwear completely exposed.

Well, I *thought* no one was paying attention, until a hand came out of nowhere and landed on my butt with a slap. And then another one. And another.

"Ouch!"

When Mikhail realized what was happening, he stopped, and with a wave of his hand, the music stopped with a thundering crash. In seconds, no one was dancing. A few people who had already started having sex were still going, and the lights were flashing like a rave in full swing, but you could have heard a pin drop.

"Who dared strike my sweet soul?" Mikhail growled.

To his credit, one of the younger Protectors, my good friend Truth, stepped forward with his hand raised. "Um, Maker, we were only following her instructions." Mikhail blinked, waiting. He knew Truth couldn't tell a lie without being violently ill. So that meant...

I sighed, trying to pull my tiny skirt down over my butt. "Growly, don't smite our friends."

Setting me down on the ground, he glared into my face. "You told them to hit you?" A few people in the crowd giggled.

I rolled my eyes, turned around, flipped up my skirt, and showed him the glitter-painted message. "It was supposed to be for you, Growly. I didn't know you were gonna have me flashing the whole Merge Two."

"Oh," he said, his cheeks becoming a darker bronze. "I, um... Apologies, everyone."

"We're not calling it The Merge Two," Hope called. She stepped up, all six feet and change of her, almost as golden as Sunny. Hope was dressed only in what appeared to be two giant feathered fans, held on by very thin chains to leave her hands free.

"Why not?" I replied.

"Because it didn't win. Everyone, make room!" She and Sunny cut through the buzzing crowd to a small, raised portion of the dance floor, and Mik and I followed them.

Hope held up an envelope, waving it until a small circle was cleared for a few feet around us. "I have the results."

Rumple, Ry, and Gavriel pushed their way to us, and we all moved so we were underneath the sign that still said *Welcome to* with a blank space.

Hope opened the envelope, pulled out a gleaming sheet of parchment, and announced, "The top five names for the new community hall were as follows. In fifth place was The Spiritual Sexposium." Everyone laughed, though a few of the crustier ex-Guides blanched slightly. "In fourth place, Heavenly Bodies."

Rumple grunted, "Fourth? Who does a Celestial have to bribe around here to get a good name chosen?"

"In third place, E-Merge-N-C Hotspot."

I snorted. "I'm not sure if that sounds like a vitamin drink or a place to charge a phone."

Hope shushed me. "In second place, The Community Consortium." A round of cheers went up from the Guides, who absolutely would pick a stupid name like that. Gavriel shot me a smug grin. I frowned at Mikhail, who was grumbling about a recount.

"Oh please, oh please, oh please," I chanted, crossing all my fingers, and then my legs. And then my eyes. "Please let it be mine."

Sunny shook her head meaningfully, and I uncrossed everything with a sigh.

Hope spoke over the excited crowd. "And now for our winner. The name of the new spiritual merging center, to be officially named by our own Maker Mikhail, is..." She handed the parchment to Mikhail, who smiled broadly as he read it silently. Then he pulled the naming chime from his robe pocket and sang the new name of the place, pointing the chime toward the sign.

"The Spiritual Cloisters!"

Everyone cheered. *Cheered.*

"What the actual fark? That was the stupidest name of them all," I muttered as the entire group sang the words together and they began to appear on the sign, as if a great invisible hand was writing them. Sunny's gaze met mine, and she crossed her eyes. At least two of us realized what a craptastic name it was.

I'd just turned away to get a drink at the bar, when the cheering died down, too quickly. "Oh shizz," Hope said, her brow crinkling.

"No, shizz would be far better than that," Gavriel muttered. Ry had slapped a hand over his mouth—trying not to laugh, I thought.

What? I thought, but no one answered me. I looked back at the sign and realized why. I read it out loud, since everyone else had gone silent. "Welcome to the Smutty Clusterfuck." Mikhail gave a wheeze when I mused, "I don't know. I like it. It's catchy."

Rumple made a strangled sound as he walked to Mikhail and took the chime. "Mik, you said it was repaired."

Mikhail glared at the chime, then at Rumple. "It was working all day, Seraphiel. I created and named a half-dozen things with it just this morning."

Rumple frowned. "What did you name today?"

"First, I created a batch of chocolate chip cookies," he started, but I stopped him with a gasp.

"You mean the cookies in our kitchen that looked exactly like chocolate chip, but turned out to be raisin? The raisins were even shaped like chocolate chips." I shuddered. "I thought Gavriel was trying to get me to eat healthy things again. I threw them away."

Sunny shivered. "Get rid of that thing, Mikhail. It's evil."

"What about the new juice glasses?" he asked, his eyebrows drawing together.

"The ones that dissolved into piles of glitter when you poured liquid into them?" Ry demanded. "I assumed they were a practical joke." His eyes darted to Rumple. He wasn't wrong to suspect Rumple; that was his sort of thing.

"I need to get back to my workshop," Mikhail muttered, his face pinched. "I made some dog toys for Shadow. I don't want him getting surprised, or hurt."

"I'll go," Gavriel offered. He'd been feeling super guilty ever since we'd moved Shadow out of Precious's room. The sweet dog had whimpered for days, and Gavriel had definitely been on Shadow's shizz list.

Perception pushed his way through the crowd and bowed slightly to Mikhail. He was sort of dressed as an angel—there was a golden pipe cleaner halo stuck on his head, anyway. Talk about phoning it in. "Maker, can I see the chime?" he asked politely.

For some reason, a Protector dressed as a fairy, wearing what looked like slightly gold-tinted plastic wrap, fluttered along behind him. I could see her nipples as clear as day right through her outfit. She'd rubbed red lipstick on them, it looked like. Or maybe raspberry sauce. Not a bad idea, actually.

"Hey, Adoration," I muttered. She didn't even glance at me. She was fluttering her eyelashes at Percy so fast, I worried she'd dislocate an eyelid.

Her voice was breathy as she spoke to Mikhail. "Yes, Maker, show it to Perception. He's so quick, so clever, I'm sure he'll see whatever it is that can be fixed." She rubbed her fingertips over his arm.

Perception didn't seem to notice. Instead, he held the chime up to the wildly changing lights and shook it a few times, humming slightly when glitter fell out. "That's unexpected."

"Ugh, I hate glitter," Adoration murmured. "No wonder

it ruined the naming ceremony. Well, glitter and that *child*."
She tutted. "We all heard what happened, of course." She
made a fake sad face and squeezed Percy's arm.

Sunny shot me a look that said three words, very clearly:
Tarp. Shovel. Hole.

I casually took the cup of beer Righteous had been
holding and stepped closer to the long-haired, hot-but-in-a-
skanky-way Protector. I leaned in. "Hey, Adoration?" I
murmured, while Perception examined the chime. She was still
touching his arm, though he kept shaking it slightly, like he'd
felt a fly land on it. "Are you okay? You're having some sort of
seizure thing there." I pointed to her face with my cup.

And then I "accidentally tripped" and spilled the beer on
her. Well, more or less spilled it. I was a lot shorter than her,
and so I had to spill it a foot and a half, upward, which took
some doing.

Bull's eye! It went right up her nose. Sunny gave me a quiet
thumbs-up.

"What the fuck?" Adoration yelled as beer dripped down
her hair and all over her costume. A glob of charcoal gray,
almost brown smut appeared on the very tip of her nose.

I giggled. "Brown noser." She stopped fluttering, shooting
me a look that was not at all adoring. Which, funnily enough,
seemed not to be good for her digestion.

"What was in the canapés?" she muttered as she let out an
enormous belch that smelled vaguely of fish.

I took a quick sniff. "Smells like sardines. Open your
mouth; I'll check again."

If looks could unmake, I'd have been exploding into glitter-sized pieces of Feather right then. Which, apparently,
wasn't any better for Adoration's intestinal situation. She let
out an enormous fart as well, which was even worse.

Perception stopped messing with the chime for long
enough to ask, "What in the world is making that stink?"

Adoration raced away, apologizing as she knocked over other guests. Sunny and I burst into gales of laughter, while Hope used one of her fans to waft away the foul air. All the people who had been standing behind Hope took a good, long look at her exposed backside while she waved.

"What's it like to have a hot wife?" I teased Sunny. Hope really was the most gorgeous woman in any realm, a walking wet dream, though I'd been told she'd shave my hair off if I kept calling her that. My Naming abilities were hard to turn off, and apparently, quite a few of the others in the Limen had started having actual wet dreams about her.

"I keep telling ya—once you go beaver, you'll never leave her," Sunny sassed, adding an exaggerated wink.

Finally, Perception handed the chime back. "Mikhail, if I had to guess"—we all grinned; guessing was what Percy did best—"I'd say the chime is working perfectly. But it's... This is going to sound nuts. Is it... Could it be playing a practical joke?"

For a moment, there was silence. Then Rumple laughed so hard, everyone jumped back. "Revel," he wheezed when he could finally speak again. "He was the one who helped me make the chime. It was his essence that went into it." He asked for the chime, humming over it slightly, his eyes glimmering as he examined it. "Revel was always the life of the party, playing jokes and teasing. This is exactly what he would do." He let out a shuddering breath. "I think Perception has it right. My little brother would definitely play this sort of joke."

I slid under Rumple's arm and hugged him. I'd seen the wetness in his eyes, and knew that even if he was smiling, he was missing his brother. We all missed him.

"So, I guess the name of this place is going to stay smutty?"

Everyone around us groaned. "I don't know, little one." Rumple handed me the chime. "Maybe you can fix it?"

I perked up at that. I would have liked to think everyone around me had full confidence in my abilities as a Namer, but at least a half-dozen Protectors sprinted for the exits, and another fifty ducked and covered like an old-fashioned tornado drill.

"Oh ye of little faith," I mumbled, holding up the chime. I sang as clearly as I could, "The Spiritual Cloisters!"

For a moment, nothing happened. But then the gold lettering began to change. We all stayed silent as the wording changed to... "The Smutty Clusterfudge?" I read aloud, and shook the chime, making more glitter fall out. "That's not an improvement."

Perception laughed. "It is, though. You know that over time, cursing adds to the imbalance. You fixed it in part, at least."

"Yeah," Sunny added. "And honestly, I think Clusterfudge is a great name."

Mikhail was still upset, though. "Spiritual Cloisters was *my* name."

"I'm sorry your sign got wrecked, Growly," I said. "Can I make you feel better?"

"I'm not sure how," he grumbled. "The chime is severely damaged; the community center has a name that I have no tools to change. If she knew of this debacle, my own Master would unmake herself in shame for having trained me—"

He stopped talking when I jumped up, grabbed him around the neck and kissed him as thoroughly as I knew how. And I'd been taking kissing lessons from four really experienced kissers for years now, so I did it well enough to distract him. "Wanna fudge?" I breathed in his ear. "We're at the Clusterfudge, after all."

"Anything for you, sweet soul," he murmured, carrying me over to the bar. My other mates gathered around.

"Are we really going to do this here?" Gavriel asked with a concerned frown.

Righteous shrugged. "I'll do anything she wants."

That was so true. He'd worn a Loch Ness monster banana hammock for an entire week after our big blow-up with Precious. After seven days of his special Nessie raising her head up out of his robe with those cute little googly eyes, looking for me, I'd pretty much gotten over my daughter telling me how much she hated me.

But the party was also a solid diversion. And lots of the Protectors were already shucking off their costumes. Rumple lifted an eyebrow. *You don't really want to stay?*

I winked, but shook my head. *I'll take a dickstraction over a distraction any day.* Although, as I thought that, two Guides found what looked like a macramé flogger and then pulled some handcuffs straight out of the wall, getting my full attention.

"A gallon of hot fudge sauce," Mikhail ordered, and the helper behind the bar picked up one of the serving buckets, along with five cups. Mikhail pushed the cups back across the bar. "To go."

"What are we doing?" I giggled as he carried me to the door, our friends shouting their farewells.

"We can cluster with fudge in our own home much more comfortably," he replied. "And it's all already set up." Gavriel, Ry, and Rumple all leaned in to give me a passionate kiss and a couple of cheeky slaps on my ass, since my underwear was apparently still giving explicit directions. Then they flew off ahead of us.

Mikhail was extremely good at multitasking, and he kissed me while we flew. And when we reached the house, he kept kissing until we were on the bed itself. Ry and Gav were in the kitchen getting more supplies, while Rumple checked on Precious.

Mikhail's glance flew in the direction of her room, and a shadow of pain crossed his face.

"Growly Bear, I'm sorry the chime is broken." I wrinkled my nose. "Well, changed, anyway."

He didn't look at me, but murmured, "I'm not worried about the chime. Well, not that worried. We have all the time in the world to fix it." His words rang with truth, but he still looked troubled. This wasn't the sort of sad that could be fixed, though. All I could do was give him something else to think about.

"What seems to be the problem, sir?" I asked breathily.

He turned back to me. While he'd been staring, I'd been taking off my nurse costume, and now wore only the stethoscope and a very naughty garter belt and fasteners.

CHAPTER 10

Mikhail

Only my sweet soul had the power to wipe away every care with a shimmy, a smile, and a promise of mischief in her emerald-bright eyes. My concerns about the damage done to the chime—even if it might not be as bad as I'd feared, as Seraphiel had assured me—were blown away as my mate approached with lust in her gaze, a stethoscope held toward me.

She pressed the end of it to my chest, listening for a moment, before tossing it to the floor beside the bed. "Your heart is perfect. But I'll need to do a thorough examination of the rest of you." Laughter spilled out of the doorway to the kitchen, as the rich aroma of hot fudge scented the air.

My eyes fell on the knotted macramé creations on the armchair nearby. "Beloved, it's not that I—"

"You're not in the mood for chocolate." Feather's soft statement held no judgment. "Or games."

I shook my head. "Not tonight, love. Can it be just you and me, for a while at least?"

"Of course."

I sent a thought to the others, gathered in the kitchen, and they all answered with understanding. I enjoyed sharing Feather with the men who were my brothers, watching her bathe in the pleasure we could provide as a group, but this month had been difficult.

Precious was almost too quick to pick up all the lessons I set for her, and never complained at the grunt work I assigned, but her spirit had been bruised, by her actions and the consequences of them.

But what hurt most was how, as soon as she had finished her work, she fled from the house as if she wanted nothing more than to escape. She rarely spoke to me, or any of us, outside of the few necessary words in my workshop or at mealtimes, though she'd taken to skipping those as well, carrying sandwiches to the edge of the Limen to eat her dinners alone.

"Maybe I should let her stop," I murmured. Feather shook her head, silver hair flying around her shoulders.

"Keep teaching her, Growly." She stood on the bed, her face almost level with mine, her hands clasping my forearms. She gripped the feathers that her other mates had given me to keep me alive, and those connections thrummed with traces of their souls' energies. "She loves us, no matter what she says."

And she will need the knowledge you impart, Seraphiel whispered in our shared connection. *It could be what will bring her back to us. It may be what tips the balance to saving her...* His voice trailed off, and I heard him leave the house.

I embraced my mate as she shivered. Seraphiel's voice had held the ring of prophecy, and it shook all her parents down to our cores to know our daughter had a terrible future awaiting her. "Kiss me, sweet soul?" Feather exhaled deeply, then lifted her eyes to mine. The love that shone from her face made me blink in wonder. "Beloved," I began, but she pressed her lips against mine, her innermost being opening almost instantly, filling the room with the perfume of roses, a silent symphony, and glittering beams of light that flew from her as she showed me her love.

As she showed me her soul.

The most beautiful soul ever created, I thought as she gently, almost reverently, removed my clothing. Her fingertips traced the scars that littered my body, lingering on the one over my heart where I had taken my flesh to make our daughter's first form.

Yes, Feather agreed, pushing me back onto the bed and lowering her naked body over me. *You* are *the most beautiful, my wonderful, talented Maker.*

She sketched a sigil for healing lightly over my heart, then drew her hands gently over my shoulders and to my wings. "These arms, these wings," she whispered, her voice filled with wonder. "So strong. And all mine." The backs of her tiny nails scraped along the edges of the leading feathers, and my cock responded, stiffening as if her hands were there instead. I held still, allowing her to dictate the speed of our lovemaking, as she threaded those hands in my hair, then downward in lazy spirals toward my groin.

I swallowed hard as she settled between my legs, blowing gently on my heated flesh. "Are you planning to torture me, beloved?"

"If making you scream and beg for more is torture? Then, yes, I am," she purred. She set her mouth to the tip of my erection, her small tongue lapping at the head so lightly it was almost imperceptible. Tasting me.

"I'll beg. I'm not proud," I groaned, fighting for control as she slowly lowered her mouth a centimeter at a time over my rigid cock. Her nipples were tight, brushing against me as she moved, her hair burning silk on my hips as she opened her mouth wider to take me in, her slender legs pressed between mine. Every movement was gentle.

Too gentle.

"More, sweet soul." Instead, she moved even more slowly, popping off the tip. "Don't you like this?" she teased. Her eyes were bright behind a messy curtain of silver hair. "Maybe I should stop. We could rest instead."

"Minx," I growled, and pushed her hair back, threading my fingers close to her scalp, then pressing her down to my cock, until her hot mouth enveloped me. I used my grip to move her over me, fucking into her mouth faster and harder than I ever had before. She took every inch as if she were starved for me, making small sounds of appreciation when I thrust even deeper.

I felt the vibration of her laugh as she sucked. *I knew I could get you to be rough with me.*

Oh, you naughty little thing, I replied, tightening my grip even more. I felt her acceptance, her pleasure, as she gave control to me. *I may give you that spanking you asked for.*

I'll take anything you want to give, my Growly Bear, she replied in my mind, her mouth too full to speak. *I trust you.*

In response, I spun out threads of my own energy, wrapping her wings in a fine mesh of light. I sent stronger cords to her most sensitive areas, to every erogenous zone I'd discovered over the years, loving the way she shivered in anticipation. Gavriel might be able to make more glorious music, and Rumple and Righteous might spin out her most decadent fantasies for her, but I was her first mate. I knew how to build her pleasure while I wrapped her in a love so pure and strong, nothing in the created universe could stand against it.

And I knew how to make her come so hard, the universe shook. I sent energy down every cord that I'd wrapped around her, and spoke a word of power that translated into *Bliss*. Her climax raced through her so quickly, she cried out around my cock, sparks of colorful glitter and electric energy rising into the air around her. I bit my tongue to keep from following her over that edge, and waited for her shuddering to lessen.

At last, she moved higher on the bed until her face was over mine, then lowered herself, sliding down over my cock. She embraced my physical form as she merged my soul with hers fully, hiding nothing. Trusting me to see and know and accept every aspect of her.

I'll love you forever, you know, she thought as she moved gently once more, slowly, both of us luxuriating in the moment. *I loved you when I was unmade in the void. I loved you when I came back. You're my foundation, my safe place. My home.*

Tears fell down our cheeks as we spiraled together in near-agonizing pleasure, and light filled the room when I pulled again at the golden threads that I'd wound around her, driving her to a peak that lasted longer than any before.

It felt like a benediction. Like a moment of silence before the ringing of a bell.

Or the calm before a hurricane of change.

Go to sleep, Growly. Tomorrow can worry about itself, Feather murmured into my mind, her small hands wrapping around my shoulders as she slipped into a favorite dream. *We've got pies to eat.*

For a moment, I slid into her fantasy, as Righteous, Seraphiel, Gavriel and I—all wearing nothing but coconut oil and judiciously placed dollops of whipped cream—stood in line to feed her an assortment of warm pastries as she sat atop a golden throne made of what appeared to be dildoes.

"More pies for your queen!" she demanded with a giggle, as we bowed.

"That's my dirty-minded little mate," I whispered, kissing her hair before leaning across the bed to retrieve the broken chime once again.

The spot on my chest where I had carved the small ball of energy to form Precious ached. I wasn't sure why, but I pressed the chime to it, murmuring the name I had given her before Feather had renamed her.

"Maker of All Things, I ask you now to keep Your eye on my daughter, the one who was once Spark of Infinite Love," I said softly. "Who became Precious, Perfect Devil, Little Glitter, shiny, and lovely, and stubborn. First and Only of her Kind; Beloved by All Realms; Guarded by the Great Gate, who was known as Revelation of Divine Mysteries—"

Before I finished speaking, the chime rang in my hand. But not with a single note, as it should. Instead, it sang out a chord, six notes that I had never heard together before, that filled me with both hope and despair.

What did it mean? I stared down at the flecks of glitter that now lay on my palm, winking as if they were waiting for me to glimpse some cosmic pattern in the ruined tool.

All will be well, dear friend, Seraphiel sent, stilling my panic, though I knew he was still across the Limen. *All will be well.*

"Pies," my sleeping mate agreed, stuffing the corner of the sheet into her mouth and chewing as she dreamed. "All will be pies."

CHAPTER 11
Precious

park. Spark. Come play.

Leave me alone, Void Boy, I thought back. *I'm not in the mood.*

Ugh. Even my thoughts sounded whiny, like I'd been crying in my mind for hours. Sure, I had been. But I knew tears never helped anything.

What helped was *power.*

I placed a hand on my chest, where I could almost feel the well of energy inside me that had been growing fast over the past month. Dad had thought he was punishing me by making me apprentice for him. But learning to make and name things had been one of my deepest dreams forever.

The true punishment had been taking Shadow away. Removing the only creature who truly understood me, who saw all the parts of me, and still loved me. I suppose, if I'd told them he wasn't just my dog, and my best friend, but also the reason I didn't hurt all the time, that his presence muted the endless pain that had been growing for the past few years, like some part of me was infected, withering inside—

"Ah!" I clutched a hand to the gap in my wing that seared with a blaze of agony for a moment.

"Woof?"

Shadow? I thought, then felt him on the other side of the wall of my bedroom. I knew my parents were all at the new sex club. Everyone was there, other than me. Even *him*. Perception, who I had loved, but now hated. He'd turned mean, his thoughts broadcast every time I was anywhere close to him.

I couldn't believe I'd wanted him. Loved him. I knew everyone else, besides my family, thought I was tainted. But Perception was supposed to be able to see clearly, to perceive the good... and the way I'd felt about him had been pure.

But the moment I'd tried to show him my thoughts, my soul, he'd wrenched himself away, and before he slammed his mental walls down, I'd caught a flash of horror in his mind.

And then I'd heard what he'd said about me to my dad, when they thought they were alone in the Merge. Well, sort of heard it. Adoration had been creeping around, skulking like she did, hoping to catch Perception alone. She had such a weak mind, with hardly any mental defenses, she'd never even noticed me listening in as she lingered at the back door of the hall.

I wished I hadn't eavesdropped, afterward. His condemnation still echoed in my nightmares.

"Nothing is safe from her these days, is it? She's a Celestial wrecking ball."

What was the big deal? I'd only kissed him once, and I'd stopped when he told me no. I mean, I hadn't tried to merge with him or anything. Even if it had felt for a split second like something had happened. Like I'd seen into his soul, and shown him a little bit of mine.

Was that why he hated me now? Had I somehow damaged him?

My mom's awkward sexplanations echoed in my memories, and I wished I could ask her about it. Talk to someone, at least, about whether or not I'd hurt him somehow. I'd never wanted to do that.

He'd called me a wrecking ball. Maybe I was one. Maybe I couldn't do anything other than ruin everything.

At first, I'd been embarrassed. Humiliated. But now, mostly, I felt rage. That was easier, anyway. I knew how to deal with anger, and use it to make myself stronger.

Hate was simple, and Perception was so easy to hate now. I'd tried to apologize, but he'd shouted for me to leave his presence the few times I'd been able to get close.

He'd made sure I saw him holding hands with Adoration.

He wanted someone like her: older, prettier, shinier. Another Protector who might someday be able to go back into the Celestial Realm with him. I would never be able to do that, not without being unmade entirely.

He was probably with her right now. Laughing. Dancing. Maybe even merging.

I wanted to burn her face off. Unmake her so completely that even the Maker of All wouldn't be able to bring her back. And I thought I might even have enough rage inside to do that.

But I hid that thought deep down, with all the other evil thoughts I'd had, and unworthy emotions.

One final, hot tear slid down my face. I wasn't anything like my parents. They were generous, good, even heroic. I would never be able to live up to their examples, no matter how hard they tried.

Perception would never want me, love me.

Spark! Come play.

The only being other than Shadow who accepted me just as I was called once more. Even though I knew it was against all the rules, even though I'd sworn not to leave, I stood and pulled on my glitter-stained overalls. What was one more broken promise at this point?

I set a hand to the wall, dipped into my well of power, and used an angelic word—with a tiny demonic inflection on the last syllable—to melt a hole just large enough for me to slip through.

An overjoyed Shadow licked my face, circled around my ankles, then ran beneath me as I flew to the Limen's edge to see my friend. "Your imaginary friend," Tata Sunny had called him since I was a toddler. But just because she couldn't see or hear him, or at least never had, didn't mean he wasn't real.

Spark? Void Boy's voice rumbled through my mind. When I was young, when I'd named him, it had been a child's voice who called me to the edge of the Limen. But now it was deeper, richer, though his body hadn't changed from what I could tell. Although, I wasn't sure if you could call a feather-shaped scrap of the void a body, exactly.

I flew up into the void, not too far, but close enough that I could feel the invisible wind brush against my wet face. *I'm here.*

Spark, who hurt you? I will unmake them for you. Each word seemed to tear into the void around him, as if he was cutting himself free to descend on the Limen and crush my enemies.

Would you crush my enemies for me, Void Boy? I teased, wiping my face and reaching out to take the edge of one tendril of his darkness in my hand. My hand went dead instantly, as it always did when I was brave enough to touch him. When I hurt enough to want to numb the pain, no matter what.

I would crush the universe for you, Little Devil, he replied. His next thought was muffled, as if he didn't want me to hear it. *In fact, I plan to.*

I ignored his threat, knowing he couldn't do it, any more

than I could really kill Adoration, or force Perception to love me back. All I could do was run away for a while, and try to stop *feeling*.

I hummed a few notes of my favorite song from the musical library Gavriel had loaned me—the one titled "Imriel's Waltz"—and put out my other hand, gasping when the void wrapped itself around me so gently, the numbness didn't even hurt.

Dance, Little Devil?

I smiled into the darkness. *I would love to.*

CHAPTER 12

Seraphiel

All will be well, I sent to Mikhail as he lay with our mate, praying that saying it might make it so.

Because what was happening before me filled me with an uncertainty I'd experienced long before, when I first flew into the void, filled with pride and hubris, determined to redeem it. To rebalance all the realms.

My daughter had flown out into the void, and as far as I could tell, was dancing with it.

Dancing with pure evil, laughing as it wrapped dark tendrils around her glittering wings. As I watched, hidden by a cloud formation, she did graceful turns and spins, the slick, deep charcoal segment of the void moving like a villainous partner around her. Seducing her.

Drawing her farther away from the Limen.

My heart raced. If she went much deeper into the void, it might be able to enfold her entirely and take her from us.

I had just opened my wings to fly over the cloud hill and after her, drawing a breath to shout, when she did a swift somersault mid-air and spun back toward the edge of our realm. "Void Boy, you're going to get me in trouble," she called out, her voice more filled with humor and light than I'd heard in years, though the tendrils kept catching at her feet and arms like tentacles. "Let me go. I promised Shadow I'd stay close."

I felt a familiar silky head tuck under my hand, and I glared down at the charcoal gray temple dog. *I am so disappointed, Shadow,* I thought. *She's not safe there.* The dog gave a sigh and stared dolefully at Precious, as if he agreed with me. I patted him, folding my wings back. *It's not time for her to go yet, Shadow. Bring her home.*

I hid myself as the hound raced out to the edge of the Limen, skidding to a stop at the very edge, his colossal paws hanging over the cloud. He opened his mouth and gave a great, baying howl.

The patch of the void that had clung to Precious shrank back, as if terrified of the sound. The Limen itself seemed to shiver. Precious sang out, "Coming!" and flew back toward our home. *Her* home.

For now, anyway.

Her steady wingbeats sounded like sand falling through an hourglass, a distant timepiece counting down the seconds. Tears stung my eyes. I'd seen what lay ahead for my sweet child, and knew I wouldn't be able to protect her. No one could, not unless we wanted all the realms to descend into the Abyss.

Please let us keep her until she's old enough to survive her future, I prayed. *Will you let her stay with us a little longer?*

I was speaking to the Mother of All, but to my shock, it was the scrap of void that answered, a sibilant hiss that slid through my mind like a serpent, the way I remembered the evil of the Abyss doing for so long. Tainting everything it touched. Leaving a burning trail of despair across my soul as it spoke.

Yessss.

Bonus Content

A Feather Kink

A Forever Feather Story

Feather

After Rumple joined us, I thought life in the Limen would be perfect. I thought I had everything a badass birch with infinite time on her hands, a world-class imagination, and access to a limitless supply of lube could need or want.

I was wrong. And I only had an hour, if that, to fix what I'd broken.

"Sunny, get in here. Please. I'm stuck," I whispered, hoping she'd come if I called to her out loud. She'd been ignoring my mental pleas for help all morning. Okay, so she and Hope were celebrating their mating anniversary, and she'd worked really hard to make the day romantic. Truth and his friends were keeping Presh and Shadow busy on the other end of the liminal realm, digging holes in the cloud ground and planting energy seeds of some kind. I was pretty sure Presh was just planting marshmallows and glitter, but even those might sprout here. The Limen was a realm without precise rules, and all sorts of weird shit kept occurring.

Like what was happening to me now. I yanked at my hair, wondering if I was going to have to cut it all off to get free.

Are you well, sweet soul? Mikhail's deep mental voice had me tugging harder. All four of my mates were at the cloud wall with Perception, listening to a report from Imriel about some old prophecy or other.

Why wouldn't I be, Daddy Bear? I answered. *You've only been gone for a few hours.*

Every hour away from you is a lifetime, my beloved.

A bead of sweat rolled down my neck. *So sweet. Love it. No need to rush home.* He sent a snippet of a love song into my mind, then dipped out, though I could feel he sensed something was up.

"SUNNY!" I shouted now, desperately hoping she would hear me. The energy privacy net Rumple had made as a gift for the two lovebirds next door was supposed to dissipate within a day, but Sunny and Hope were obviously eking out every last minute they could before Presh came home. Shrieking out, more like. I was pretty sure I'd heard moaning even through the net.

Sunny, I need you. It's live or die.

When she answered at last, she was not amused. *What the fudge, girlfriend? This better be an emergency.*

It is, I thought back, and sent her a mental image of what had happened.

"Oh, shit," she muttered not two minutes later, staring down at me. Her dark brown skin was extra shiny, and her hair fell in perfect curls around her face. Her laughing face. "How in the name of all the realms did you manage this, birch?" She snorted and put her hands on her hips, shaking her head slightly. "I gotta tell Hope to come see this."

I glared up at her the best I could with my hair glued to the sheet beneath me. "A true friend wouldn't mock. She would keep this moment secret. She would honor the sanctity of our friendshi— Oh, hi, Hope."

"Goodness, Feather, that looks terribly awkward." Hope

glided across the room, something in her hands. Probably scissors, to cut me free. I was about to thank her, when I saw a flash of light, and had to blink away the residual starbursts.

"What was that?" I demanded, as she leaned over Sunny's shoulder, kissed her, then showed her the thing that had flashed. *Wait.* "If that is a camera, so help me—"

"It is," Hope chirped, tossing her long blonde hair over one shoulder. She had on a golden miniskirt and bandeau top that made her look like the universe's top supermodel, but the gleam in her eyes was all post-sex bliss. Well, that and the mischief she only showed when she was around Sunny. I sort of loved it. "I got Perception to help me create this out of some of the power pools. It takes a likeness *with* auras, and shows the emotions the subject was feeling. I'm doing an exhibit, and I needed embarrassment and humiliation to round out the show. Thanks, sweets!" She gave Sunny another kiss and glided out of the room. "I recommend peanut butter," she called over one bare shoulder before the door closed.

"Hope the Wet Dream, I will rain the void down on you if you show that picture to anyone!" I yelled back, slightly too late.

"Shush," Sunny chided. "Let me get you out. Peanut butter, huh? So is this chewing gum in your hair, birch?"

"No," I complained, pulling my knees up underneath me. "It's fudge sauce, caramel... and a little hot glue."

"What were you *doing?*" she asked as she went to the next room where we kept our food. Nothing actually spoiled in the Limen, but with the five of us living in this house, having as much sex as we did, it didn't make sense to drag ourselves down to the Limenteria every day to eat. It cut into prime merging time.

I practiced my breathing exercises while Sunny rattled around, looking for the jar of peanut butter. "Why do you have fourteen bottles of chocolate sauce, and almost as much caramel?" she called.

"You know why," I replied as she came back, carrying a jar of peanut butter.

"Because you and your guys are a bunch of hungry sex fiends." She unscrewed the jar as she crossed the room. "Hope's probably right. This trick worked for chewing gum in my hair on Earth, so I guess it should be fine for caramel and fudge sauce here. The hot glue is a problem, though."

"Don't ask me how I know, but lube works on hot glue," I muttered. "There's some—"

"In the fifty-five-gallon drum," she finished for me with an aggrieved sigh, pulling the golden cloth off what a casual observer might believe was a bedside table. I heard the squirt of the golden spigot, a soft curse, and then felt Sunny's hands in my hair, full of peanut butter and lube. "Here." She slapped another handful of lube into my palm. "We have a few extra minutes; Hope is running interference with Ry and Mik at the wall. Did you hear what's going on in the Celestial Realm?"

"No," I said, rubbing the lube over my matted hair. "What's Imriel saying this time? Are we wrecking the balance and need to pray seventeen hours a day instead of sixteen? Is it time for another energy fast? Or power enemas, or whatever his thing was last time?" We both giggled.

"At least he's laid off Presh for the moment," Sunny muttered, as the lube worked on the glue. "Perception turned her classes over to the Guides, and she's being trained in all the traditional Protector subjects."

"How's she taking that?" I met Sunny's eyes, and she shrugged.

"She's obsessed with Percy. It makes him so uncomfortable. It's probably good for both of them to get some distance." I hummed my agreement. "Now, birch, tell me exactly what you were doing here."

I pulled my last handful of hair free of the mess and stared down at my sheets with deep sadness. It would take a while to get them clean, and they were my favorite two-million-thread-count set. "I wanted to spice things up in the bedroom," I admitted, following Sunny through to the bathroom, where she filled the tub while I explained. "All of them have these wild experiences—even Ry has done stuff that I didn't even know was possible."

"Do they make you feel bad about being less experienced?" she snapped out, tapping one hand with a bristled foot brush. "Because if they do, I will help straighten them out."

"No." I grinned. "They like debauching me. But I want to add more to our group."

"Tired of the tentacles already?" She wiggled her eyebrows.

I licked my lips as I climbed into the bath. "Rumple's tentacles are my fifth mate, Sunny. I'll never get tired of them."

She curled her lip, jealous as she should be of my Rumple's Celestial gifts. Although his memories were supposedly the gift the Maker of All had given him when he walked through the gate, She'd also thrown me a bone by letting him keep my favorite parts—the horns, tail, and forked tongue—and by tossing in adjustable tentacles on top of it all.

She was a loving Creator, after all.

"No, Sunny," I continued as I ran a comb through my tangled hair. "I was trying to hot glue the sheets up to the walls and build an omega nest for real. I had pillows and mood lighting, scented oils, everything ready. And I've been prac-ticing making energy knots to stick at the bases of all their co—"

She yelled, "TMI!" to make me stop.

I winked. "Anyway. I thought I could use the caramel sauce as my omega slick... but it spilled, and there was a jar of hot fudge left opened from last night, and the glue gun slipped, and I got caught up..."

"What possessed you, Feather?" Her eyes widened. "*Are* you possessed? Is it the void rabies again?"

"I told you a million times, I don't have void rabies, or void scabies, or void gonorrhea." I stuck my tongue out when she scoffed. "Anyway, it's not them. It's me. I already wrote my book of fantasies years and years ago, and we did all those."

"Yeah, and the Limen is still recovering," she interrupted, but I frowned her to silence.

"I need something... new." I held up a hand. "We've done chocolate sauce, caramel, role play as pirates, firefighters, and Nobel scientists. We've done all the positions, and all the major kinks. A few of the minor ones, too." I let out a chuckle; I had a feeling she and Hope were still enjoying the leftover kitten costumes Rumple had whipped up when I'd wondered aloud what the whole deal with furries was.

"I think maybe what you need is something old, not new," she said after a long moment. "The oldest, most sacred sensual exercise. I'll even loan you the supplies."

I wasn't the slightest bit shocked when she ran home and came back, while I was still getting dressed in my *Rumple These Sheets, Sir* glitter-painted toga, carrying a basket full of thick yarn.

"What is it with you people and macramé?" I groused as she dumped the basket out next to the bed. "I mean, I like rope-play as much or more than the next kinky sex fiend. But this yarn is so gross."

Sunny grabbed fresh sheets while I organized the balls of yarn. As she remade the bed, she explained, "It's not the yarn. It's the meditation you do while you're knotting it." I wrinkled my face up, confused, and she sighed. "Here." She put her hands on my cheeks, squeezing. "I'm going to show you the theory behind sacred macramé, and then you will shock your mates with this kind of knotting. Not the Alpha kind."

"But I like Alpha knots. Or the idea of them. And Mikhail is really, really good with changing the shape of his sausage anyway, so it's not like it would be hard to really get into it," I grumbled as she began to fill my mind with a whole ton of images.

In less than five minutes, I was blinking up at her. She had her superior, "I know more than you about merging" expression on. Which she totally deserved.

She knew *a lot* more than I did.

"That's... wild," I whispered, still trying to cope with all she had shown me.

"Told ya," she sang. "Now your mates will be here soon. You've got five colors of yarn. Get knotting, babe."

"Sweet soul?" Mikhail called out when the front door opened. "What's that smell?"

"Oh, Goddess, tell me she hasn't been cooking again," Righteous mumbled, then exhaled sharply. I was almost certain Gavriel had punched him in the stomach.

Good. Honestly. You burn ten or twelve batches of brownies, and suddenly everyone is like, "She's a menace in the kitchen."

"Imp?" Rumple crooned from the bedroom doorway. His golden horns almost scraped the doorframe, and he had to fold his wings tightly to get inside. He stepped carefully around the patterns of yarn on the floor. "Who gave you this delicious idea, little one?"

His whirling golden eyes took in the four towel-holder-looking things I'd made and placed on the floor. One was knotted in the shape of a turtle, more or less. Another was a rabbit, the next one was a butterfly, and the last one, which Rumple reached down to pick up, was an octopus.

"Stop!" I yelled. "That one's not yours!"

His smile grew so broad, the room lit up with holy fire. "Little imp, did you really... did you knot these with intention? Is this holy macramé? I had no idea you understood the theory behind this art. It's so advanced."

He sounded so impressed, awestruck even, that I didn't tell him Sunny had given me the instructions. Well, mostly. I'd improvised a little on the octopus.

"You know not to touch it yet," I warned, holding up the energy ring I'd made that would be attached to all the yarn creations. "Once I have the ring juiced up all the way, you'll each get to touch the one intended for you."

His eyes widened in appreciation. "I'm not the octopus?" he asked, curiosity filling his expression with mischief. "Color me intrigued."

"Why does it smell like peanut butter in here?" Gavriel demanded, flinging himself onto the bed. "Have you been stress-baking again, Nemesis?"

I growled at him, and felt him ruffling through my thoughts. He'd been doing this more often, trying to teach me how to close off my thoughts to others. Sneak attacks were his favorite teaching method. He caught a quick memory of Sunny helping me get my hair free, and the omega nest idea before I shoved him out. "Rude, Gavriel. See if I let you be part of my macramé project."

His jaw dropped. "How did you learn macramé?"

I was starting to feel slightly pissed off about the whole thing. *Wow, Grumpy,* I snarked mentally. *You'd think I'd never done something really impressive, like, I don't know, created a giant mandala of energy that was literally redeeming the void around us a particle at a time with the reflections off the glitter—*

I have only ever been impressed by you, my beloved antago-nist, Gav whispered into my mind, opening his soul slightly so I could see how deep his love was. *At everything you do. Who you are. How you love.*

"I know," I replied, feeling churlish, and wrestled with the last knot on my energy ring.

But when Righteous entered the room, his large white wings flexing almost as hard as his finely honed man-breasts, and asked, "Why the hell would you want to do macramé, Scrap?" I blew him a kiss.

"For one reason alone," I said, standing up and holding the energy ring for them to see. "Kink."

Stepping through the doorway to join us, Mikhail snorted. "That's my girl." He moved in front of me, examining my yarn creations on the floor. "I'm more than ready to be at your mercy, sweet soul. Which one is mine?"

I giggled. "Which one do you think?"

He started to lean toward the turtle, but then frowned. "I honestly don't know, love."

"Well, mine is the rabbit," Righteous announced. "Because I can hop and hop all over that delectable little body and never stop coming, right, Scrap?"

I snorted at the grim expressions on my older mates' faces. Ry's refractory time was actually ridiculously impressive. Sometimes I'd swear he could come *while* he was coming. Like an Oreo of orgasms, one on top of the other. A club sandwich of climaxes. A millefeuille of—

"Focus, Nemesis," Gavriel snapped. "Who gets to be the octopus?"

He had a wicked gleam in his eyes, and I curled my lip at him. "You get to be the rabbit, Gavriel." Rumple and Mikhail both burst into laughter at that, leaving Ry looking confused. "You're the turtle, Head Boy," I said, pointing him toward the green turtle.

He scowled down at it. "Why?"

Gavriel sighed and stepped toward the rabbit. "Macramé is a teaching tool as well as a merging technique. In this exercise, we'll be adopting sexual merging traits that are not our strongest suit. Is that right, little wretch?"

I stifled a laugh, pointing Rumple to the butterfly. "This may kill me," he said, staring at the fragile, loosely knotted wings. "I won't be able to feel almost... anything. Touch you with any sort of..."

"Oh, shit," Ry breathed, staring at the turtle in horror.

Mikhail let out a huge laugh, and grabbed the octopus. "Well, I've always wondered what those tentacles of Rafe's feel when they're inside you. I suppose I'm about to find out."

I nodded, and held the ring out. "Snap your towel holder ends—"

"Haloes," Rumple interrupted. "They're haloes. Not towel holders."

"Snap your towel haloes onto mine, and let's get this party started."

In less than a minute, they had each connected their macramé creations to my halo of energy, and I'd placed it on the wall over the bed. It looked like some hideous alien craft form, but the energy that it was already generating was astounding.

"What's happening to me?" Righteous yelped, staring down at his groin. "It's getting... smaller." His panicked gaze met mine.

Oh, crapola. Had I shrunk Ry's anaconda?

We both looked to Rumple, who was laughing so hard he'd fallen over onto the bed. Which did not budge a bit. It was as if a butterfly had landed on the sheet, with no weight. His voice was light and soft as he answered, "No, sweet Righteous. Your cock is fine. It's just... turtling."

Ry scowled. "Is this like the time you did that docking

thing with me? That was fun, but I'm pretty sure I can't do it alone..."

"No, no, oh crap, what is happening, no," Gavriel interrupted, his words falling over each other quickly as he paced near the base of the bed. He was jittery, almost. Like he'd just slammed a bunch of energy drinks. I licked my lips at him, and his eyes went wide. "Get in the bed right now, Feather, or I'm going to come all over— *Shit*." He slammed a hand over his trousers. He hadn't managed to get them off, but there was already a big, wet stain there.

"Don't swear that's never happened before, Gav," Mikhail teased as he slid up onto the bed beside me. At some point while the others were messing around, he'd gotten naked, and I admired his bronze body, decorated with ever-diminishing silver, sickle-shaped scars. Golden ropes of energy were wrapping around his waist, and I noted they had little suckers on them. As he pulled me into his arms and kissed me deeply, his tongue thrusting into my open mouth, those tentacles began exploring my body below. They were slightly cooler than my own skin, and they latched on, sucking a little bit at each end, as they moved all around my abdomen, and then down, pulling my lower lips apart and sliding through my already damp folds.

"How many tentacles do you think you can take?" Mikhail growled in my ear. "Without my cock inside you?"

Not waiting for an answer, he slid one, then two, into me, and began moving them in and out, the small suckers setting up a strange sort of percussive suction inside me. When one attached to my G-spot and pulsed somehow, at the same time another one pulled on my clit from outside, I felt a sharp, unexpected climax rock my body.

"I want you," I complained as I came down from my release, but Mikhail only held me open, allowing more and more golden tentacles to fill me. He didn't answer, and almost seemed beyond speech.

"Shush, love," Rumple answered for him. "Let Mikhail play." Then Rumple began kissing me, but his lips on mine were so soft it felt like the flutter of tiny wings. Tantalizing, and gentle, and for some reason, it brought tears to my eyes. "This is what it felt like, when you touched me that first time, in Sanctuary," he whispered. "My armor kept me from feeling you fully. It was so soft, so gentle. So perfect." His hand threaded through my hair, and I closed my eyes at the simultaneous gentle touch above, and less gentle one below.

Then the tentacles withdrew, and Mikhail's thick girth replaced them, his massive hands under my hips, lifting me partly off the bed. I sighed into the blissful sensation, pressing my small wings and shoulders back on my superfine sheets as he began to thrust.

"I'm not sure this is enough," Mikhail grumbled, his hands now gripping my hips almost roughly. I blinked up at him. His eyes were almost fevered, as if the energy I'd gifted him with in the macramé was possessing him somehow. "I want to stuff you so fucking full, you'll feel me inside you for weeks," he growled, and I felt those grasping, phantom limbs begin to move inexorably closer to my pussy. And then, one after another, while he was still thrusting inside me, they began to dip inside as well, sliding alongside his erection, making the stretch unbelievably wide.

It's a good thing you've learned to take Ry's anaconda, imp. Rumple's mental thread was as soft as his lips on mine. *But I wonder if Mikhail will test your boundaries in another—*

I stopped listening, because I felt one of those tentacles move lower and begin to slide slowly into my ass. "Holy hand grenades," I muttered as another one joined it, the two twining around each other and setting up an alternating rhythm with

Mikhail's fucking. My building orgasm was almost terrifying in its intensity, as Mikhail's soul opened, and I felt what the linking of his energy to my halo had done. Mikhail was always gentle with me. Sometimes too gentle, pushing the others to back away from exploring things I might like to try, if only once.

But now, the holy intention—that's how Sunny had phrased it—of the prayer I'd woven had imbued his soul with a hint of recklessness. Not of violence, but a darker lust.

When another tentacle breached my ass, I shuddered at the fierce expression on my usually gentle mate's brow. "Take it, sweet soul. Take it all; take all of me." He reached up and grasped one of my nipples, rolling it roughly between two fingers, until I cried out. At that same moment, a tentacle slapped over my clit and pulled hard on it... and another, longer one somehow reared up behind my back, and found the feather at my nape, forcing a whip of pleasure through it.

The world exploded as I opened my soul to Mikhail's psychic ravishment, and we both came and came, our essences entwining to a level I wasn't sure I'd ever felt.

We spiraled down slowly. Rumple had backed away, and Mikhail kissed me now, his gaze strangely vulnerable. "Was that... I didn't hurt you, did I, my beloved?" he asked at last.

I grasped his chin in my hands, forcing his gaze to mine. "Not even a little," I promised. "That was gorgeous. Glorious." I smiled as the fear receded from his turquoise and black eyes. "I mean, I may not want to fuck you plus a dozen tentacles *every* day." I shifted on the sheets. "But maybe once a week?"

He growled and took my mouth in a long, deep kiss. "Anything you ask, my dearest love," he said, whispering the vow into my mouth. "All you need to do is think it, and I will make it happen."

My thoughts flickered to my other mates, and Mikhail

smiled, gently moving off the bed. "Gavriel? Righteous? I think she needs you."

"Yes, sir," Righteous said, rushing across the room.

Rumple huffed a laugh, and he swatted Ry's bare ass when he pushed past my horned lover. "You calling everyone sir now, sweet boy?"

Righteous blushed an adorable deep gold, and bit his lower lip. I rubbed my thighs together, as turned on as I always was by the dynamic between my oldest and youngest mates. "No, sir," Ry answered breathlessly, and Rumple smiled widely.

"You'd better get that anaconda—no, that turtle of yours —to work, sweetness," Rumple purred. "It's going to take you a very, very long time to climax."

"Yes, sir," Ry said again, but his attention was on me. For a moment, I was lost in his eyes. The love in them was as fresh and perfect as it had been for years now. I let my hands move over his mating marks, liking the soft grunts and gasps from the others as they felt the sensations as well.

Then I put my own fingers around my right breast and tightened my grip, pinching the areola and Ry's mating feather, and working my way to the nipple. "I need you, Ry," I begged. "Please get inside me."

"Yes, Scrap." He put the head of his cock up to my entrance. "I love feeling this," he whispered in my ear as he began to slide inside. "Love feeling you full of one of your other mates' release, sliding through it. So wet and hot inside you. Someday I want to take your ass, love. I'll wait until the others have come inside you, loosened you up. Opened you for me. Filled you full of their heat, their come. I'll fuck into it, fill you so full you're aching." He thrust a bit harder as he spoke, his filthy words mingling with even more graphic dirty thoughts as he pictured bending me into a dozen positions, and owning every part of my body.

I came, but when I'd only just stopped shuddering from that orgasm, Gavriel was there, holding his cock to my mouth. "Suck it, *please*, Feather," he begged. His features were almost distraught. "It burns."

"Burns?" I glanced at Mikhail and Rumple, but they were sitting in cloud chairs lazily stroking their cocks, and they both laughed.

"He's not hurt, beloved," Mik said. "He's just horny. Rabbits come fast, and often. I think he's pent up already. Better help him out." I opened my mouth, relieved, and felt Gavriel's smooth, long cock on my tongue. I hadn't done more than suck him four to five times when I felt his hot release in the back of my throat and swallowed him down. I loved the way Gavriel tasted, ever so slightly of mint and salted honey.

"More," I demanded, and he sighed, but his cock was already hardening again. I sucked him a little longer this time —maybe a minute—before he was in the grip of a second, more powerful orgasm. He pulled out then and started to move off the bed, but I licked my lips. "No, stay." Ry's consistent pounding inside my pussy was pushing me toward a deeper orgasm, and I wanted to feel them both coming inside me at the same time. "Do that thing where you connect inside?" I pleaded.

Gavriel smiled indulgently. "Only if Righteous consents."

Righteous had already shouted a loud *yes* into both our minds, though, and when Gavriel entered my mouth again, he snuck a narrow thread of his soulfire inside as well. Righteous responded, and I felt a long, thin thread moving through me —looping loosely around my clit on the way up. When the two threads met in my core, Gavriel's energy was, as usual, stronger than Ry's. My youngest mate's soul flew wide, every thought and fantasy and dream exposed.

"Fuck, I love this part," Rumple said with a groan, suddenly behind Righteous. "Sweet boy, let me in?"

Righteousness was beyond words; Gavriel's soul was inside his, moving through Ry's vessel at the same rapid pace his own cock moved in my mouth. Fucking me physically, and Ry spiritually.

"Yes, sir. Please, Rafe," Ry managed to say, and I felt Rumple move behind his body. I couldn't see what they were doing; I wasn't sure if they were physically merging, but Righteous bit his lip and let out a small cry of pleasure, so I knew Rumple had invaded at least the outer wall of his soul.

Ry lay closer, pressing down on top of me, as Rumple kissed along the back of his neck, then moved his lips to my arms, licking and exploring my sensitive skin with his forked tongue. He was thrusting gently, and I caught Righteous's gaze with mine. His was almost tormented.

"Ry, are you okay?"

"He's inside me, Feather," he groaned as he pounded into me slowly, that huge cock stretching my walls. "He's inside me, his cock is in me, but it's ephemeral. I can almost not feel him. Like a dream, like a fantasy."

"Let me feel?" I asked, and Ry nodded, the blush in his cheeks growing deeper as he opened his senses to mine, and we bound them together.

It was just as he had said, Rumple's cock almost a shadow, rather than physical reality. So hard, strong, yet gentle. It matched the love he felt for us all.

For me.

These men would give me anything I wanted, they loved me so much. And I would do the same. I opened my soul to them all, feeling the humming of my name song, and theirs, and the song of love, resonating and amplified in the halo that was up on the wall over the bed.

Gavriel moaned. "I can't stop coming," he said with a

groan, and filled my mouth with his sweet release. I swallowed him down, again and again as his orgasms began to cascade over him, drowning him in pleasure.

"Now, Ry," Rumple commanded, and Righteous thrust one more time, as deeply as possible. We all came: Rumple, Ry, Gav, me... and from the sound of it, and the searing pleasure in my nape, Mikhail as well, in his chair.

Ry collapsed on top of me, laughing softly. I ran my fingers through his shaggy dark hair, and whispered my love into his ear. Mikhail and Gavriel rose and brought warm cloths to the bed, then the three oldest mates cleaned Righteous and me, praising us both.

Well, praising and stroking. Gavriel was still coming every minute or two. From the look in his eye, and the way he ran a hand over my stomach, like he was seeing how full it was getting, I had almost decided that he might have an inflation kink.

"I have a Feather kink," he corrected, pulling me into his arms. The others arranged themselves around me, and we lay there while Gavriel and Rumple sang a duet that somehow brought us all together even closer.

"A Feather kink?" I asked as sleep threatened to pull me under. "Is there such a thing?"

"Oh yes," one of them replied, though I wasn't sure who. I smiled as I fell into a dream, under the holy macramé, in the arms of my lovers, who were all thinking the same thing.

I definitely *have a Feather kink.*

Hmmm. Maybe life in the Limen was perfect after all.

The End

Also by Merri Bright

Want to check out Merri's other series?

The Billionaire's Betasitter - mf, omegaverse, contemporary, grumpy/sunshine, age gap romcoms.

Sunshine's Grump

The Lost Lines Series - why choose, omegaverse, historical fantasy.

Vali's Stories:

The Omega's Mischief: A Short Story Prequel

The King's Omega: The Lost Lines Series Book 1

The Queen's Nest: A Lost Lines Series Novella

Haven's Story:

The Guards' Haven

Roya's Story:

The Assassin's Promise: The Lost Lines Series Book 2

Wren/Angel's Story:

The Leviathan's Debt: The Lost Lines Series

Acknowledgments

The deeper into a series I get, the more help I need to keep from sailing off into the continuity void. Thank you to the Glitterati (Courtney, Liza, Maria, Bekka, Megan, Alex, and Lucila) and to Deb, Heartsnarker, Sarah, and Indie for helping make this novella shine.

Thank you to Kate Farlow for the incredible cover, Raewyn Ash for the fast and fabulous editing, and Darcy Bennett for the constant supply of Henry Cavill pics, filthy/funny memes, and common sense advice.

Readers, you have given me some of my best days ever this year. Thank you for sharing your love for my smutty little angel.

About the Author

Merri Bright writes stories filled with magic, since those are the books she loves to read. She spends her days dreaming about naughty angels, misunderstood demons, sexy shifters, growly Alpha males, and frequently refuses to limit her heroines to just one love interest.

Please join Merri's Mischief Makers on Facebook where you'll discover random giveaways, sneak peeks of new novels, book recommendations, and silly/sexy/funny stuff. Or email her at merri@merribright.com.